A FINE ROMANCE

He watched as she walked towards the block of flats. From a distance, she looked lonely and vulnerable, and he experienced a sudden pang of regret. Maybe one of them should have tried harder. He started to open the van door, but then remembered it was stuck. Hastily, he clambered over the wicker chair and jumped out on the other side. He raced up to the building but, by the time he reached the lobby, Laura had disappeared from view and the automatic doors were locked against him. He scanned the rows of nameplates but foolishly recalled that he didn't even know her name.

He shrugged and walked slowly back to his van. He climbed in and slammed the door behind him. As he drove away, defeated, into the night, the handle fell off and landed with a dull clank in the gutter.

A Fine Romance

BOB LARBEY

Adapted from the television series
by Trisha Marshall

ARROW BOOKS

Arrow Books Limited
17–21 Conway Street, London W1P 6JD

An imprint of the Hutchinson Publishing Group

London Melbourne Sydney Auckland
Johannesburg and agencies throughout
the world

First published 1983

Characterization & format © Bob Larbey
Novelization © Trisha Marshall

Phototypeset in Linotron Baskerville by
Input Typesetting Ltd, London

Made and printed in Great Britain
by The Anchor Press Ltd
Tiptree, Essex

ISBN 0 09 9326701

To Humphrey Barclay

I

Laura Dalton's proudest boast was that, at thirty-nine, she was younger than Jane Fonda, but, although she said it as a joke, a quiet desperation was occasionally discernible in her voice. She was, as they say in all the best Hollywood movies, 'homely' and, even though she had discarded her glasses in favour of contact lenses, no man had ever said to her, 'Gee but you're beautiful, Miss Dalton.'

Mike Selway was forty-three, short and unprepossessing. When it came to meeting the opposite sex he could be diffident to the point of rudeness. This wasn't at all intentional on his part, nor was it some fiendish masculine ploy, he was just chronically shy.

Laura met Mike, not exactly by chance, at a party given by Laura's sister, Helen. Whereas Laura was unremarkable in looks and confidence, her younger sister was effortlessly attractive and easy going. Happily married to Phil, a handsome and rising young executive, Helen lived an Ideal Life in an Ideal Home environment. The sisters were close, but Helen had one annoying habit as far as Laura was concerned, and that was trying to match her up with the right bloke. Match-making seemed to be a hobby with happily married people, Laura noticed. It was almost as if they felt some kind of evangelical duty to persuade non-believers to convert to their perfect way of life. Helen had been solely responsible for some disastrous mis-matches in the past – the Danish dentist sprang immediately to mind: he had perfect teeth (always a sinister sign) and the whip above his bed confirmed Laura's worst fears.

Phil was a convivial chap, but lately he was beginning to dread Helen's parties because they seemed to revolve inexorably around his sister-in-law and her non-existent love-life. On the night of this particular party, Helen was in a state because her carefully chosen partner for Laura had called off at the last minute. It was Phil who suggested his friend Mike as a replacement. Helen thought that he definitely wasn't her sister's type but reluctantly settled for second best; with Laura it was becoming a case of any port in a storm.

As it turned out, Helen's misgivings were well founded: the meeting between Mike and Laura was not exactly an auspicious one. In fact, it was nothing short of disastrous.

The party was going with a swing – for everyone, that is, except Laura, who was wandering around aimlessly with a plate of sausages. Resorting to domestic details was always Laura's standby on these occasions and, by the time everyone else was merry and relaxed, she would be in the kitchen surrounded by stacks of washing-up. The dirty glasses were just beginning to accumulate nicely when she caught sight of Helen and Phil heading remorselessly towards her. Before she could retreat to the kitchen, she found herself face to face with a short, nondescript man with tousled hair, rumpled clothes and a slightly crazed expression in his eyes.

Then came the dreaded words of introduction: 'Laura, meet Mike,' Helen said brightly – rather too brightly for Laura's liking.

'Hello – hello,' Mike responded automatically, swivelling his head stiffly from side to side in acknowledgement.

Laura looked at Mike and didn't like what she saw.

8

He put her in mind of a ventriloquist's dummy. His grin had now set firmly on his face and he seemed to be looking at something over her left shoulder.

'Laura's my sister,' Helen said, endeavouring to get the conversation flowing.

'So . . .' Mike said vaguely – now looking at something over Laura's *right* shoulder. For the life of him he couldn't think of anything else he wanted to say and so decided to extend his smile instead. By this time Laura was beginning to think that, just like the Cheshire cat, he would soon disappear completely, leaving his weird and unnerving grin hanging in the air.

Helen nudged Phil, who seemed to be finding the whole thing rather amusing.

'What are you drinking, Mike?' he asked.

Mike was by now so mesmerized with nerves that he wasn't attending to what anyone was saying. 'Please,' he responded automatically.

Phil decided to let this elliptical remark pass and went off to fix his friend a stiff drink.

'Laura's a linguist,' said Helen, giving Mike his cue.

'Oh,' said Mike, neglecting to follow it up.

'Somewhat,' said Laura tersely.

'*Bon*,' riposted Mike.

'*Oui*,' Laura said flatly.

This gave Mike the necessary inspiration. 'Excuse me. Loo,' he said urgently, and hurried away.

Hopeless, Laura thought, and eyed Helen. 'Why on earth do you keep trying to fix me up when I don't want you to?'

'Why on earth should you think that?' bluffed Helen.

'He comes through the door. You grab him, plough his through the crowd like a harvester through a field of corn, and introduce him to *me*, that's why!'

'I just want you to be as happy as Phil and I,' said Helen rather touchingly.

'Helen,' said Laura tiredly, 'life is not *like* you and Phil.'

'At least try.'

'With him?' Laura scoffed.

'He's not that awful.'

'No? As far as I can see, he's a monosyllabic dwarf with a fixed grin and a weak bladder.'

Upstairs, the monosyllabic dwarf with the fixed grin and the weak bladder had deliberately locked himself in the lavatory. An unexpected and welcome diversion had been provided by a giant crossword pinned to the back of the door and he was now halfway through his sixth clue. Unfortunately for Mike, his rather unoriginal hiding place had been sussed out by Phil, and he soon found himself being propelled back downstairs.

'Phil must have broken down the door of the loo,' Laura remarked sarcastically as she caught sight of Mike's panic-stricken face.

'Ah, Mike, there you are!' Helen said, trying to compensate for her sister's obvious lack of enthusiasm.

'Yes,' said Mike.

Laura was finding this man's charm distinctly underwhelming.

'Will you please utter more than one syllable!' she snapped.

He took a step backwards in surprise. 'Yes. All right,' he stuttered.

'Thank you,' said Laura and glared at him.

Obviously feeling that the couple were making an important breakthrough in conversational technique, Helen suggested that they both sit down together and have a chat.

'No, well, if Laura's going to wash up . . .' Mike

said hopefully, looking at the trayful of glasses Laura was clutching grimly to her chest.

Helen swiftly snatched the tray away.

'What would you like to drink?' Mike asked tentatively.

'Gin and tonic, please.'

'Right,' said Mike and turned to go, but Phil was on to him in a flash.

'I'll get them,' he said, and disappeared before Mike could argue.

Mike sighed. He was stuck with her now. 'Where would you like to sit?'

'On a seat,' said Laura, determined to give this graceless idiot no help whatsoever, in the hope that he would take the hint and go away. With Helen hovering around, however, escape for either of them was proving impossible.

'There, there! Sit there!' she almost shouted, and directed their two stiff little bodies towards a nearby sofa.

'You're taller than I thought you were,' Laura remarked, looking him up and down.

'So are you,' Mike said, returning the insult.

Phil arrived with two glasses of gin and a bottle of tonic. 'Right, that's you two fixed up,' he said with some considerable relief as he put the drinks down on a side table.

Helen gave him an exasperated glare and he realized he had come up with the wrong phrase at the wrong moment. 'I didn't mean . . .' He started to apologize and then gave up. 'Oh, sod it!' Shaking his head, he went off to rejoin the party and normality.

Giving the couple a smile of encouragement, Helen turned away. Wedged on the sofa, Mike and Laura smiled warily at each other.

'Let's have a drink,' Laura suggested, picking up the bottle of tonic.

'No, let me do that,' Mike insisted, taking the bottle from her.

As soon as he tried to turn the screw top, he knew he was a doomed man. It wouldn't budge. Hating the inevitability of it all, he wrestled manfully for a second or two. The palm of his hand was beginning to sting.

'I need a cloth. A hankie!' he said, putting the bottle down and rummaging through his pockets.

Casually, Laura picked up the bottle and opened it effortlessly. One quick look at Mike's face made her wish she hadn't. Resignedly he held out his glass and allowed her to pour the tonic. They sipped their drinks in silence. Everywhere they looked they were surrounded by garrulous partygoers happily engaged in witty conversation.

'I think companionable silences are a myth,' Laura remarked.

'I talk too much sometimes,' Mike said.

She looked at him incredulously. 'Really?'

'Yes. Particularly with strangers,' said Mike, seemingly unaware of the sarcasm in her voice. 'I start talking without really knowing what I'm going to say, but I keep talking . . . Then I start to hear the sound of my own voice as if it's echoing in a tunnel, but I keep talking. The last party I went to, I got on to a wall.'

'Not literally?'

'No. The subject of a wall I'd been putting up in this fellow's garden. I'm a landscape gardener, you see. Anyway, I got on to the subject of this wall and I couldn't get off it. The fellow kept changing his mind, you see. First of all he wanted Cotswold stone, then Derbyshire stone – then he thought he'd have screen-walling – during which time I was going slowly bananas.'

Aren't we all? thought Laura, stifling a yawn.

'Well, finally he settled for Cotswold,' Mike droned

on, 'which of course needs to be laid in the half-bond manner. No, he didn't want that, so I said to him, "Look, the half-bond manner is the only way . . ."' He tailed off, aware that Laura was slightly less than riveted by this gardening monologue. 'And I can hear the sound of my own voice in that tunnel again,' he said apologetically. He could feel himself getting hot and sticky under the collar and cast around forlornly for something witty to say. The woman was staring at him as if he were mad and in an effort to distract her attention he said desperately, 'You. Let's talk about you. Helen said you were a linguist.'

'Minor.'

Mike ventured a little joke. 'Oh. Surface work or at the coal-face?'

He received a stony stare.

'Sorry,' he apologized. 'A minor linguist. And what do you do for a living?'

'Linge.'

'Sorry – '

'I translate things. It's all pretty boring.'

'Oh, I'm sure it's not. What are you translating at the moment?'

'A German textbook about urinary infections.' This was said with some satisfaction at having proved a point.

'Oh.'

'There's always sex,' Laura said.

Beginning to wonder what he had let himself in for, Mike stared at her in embarrassment.

'To talk about, I mean,' she said. 'That's always common ground.'

'Oh, sure,' Mike said, giving an inward sigh of relief. 'Every party conversation gets round to it sooner or later.'

'Always.'

Neither one of them, however, felt capable of

opening the batting on the sexual front, and there was another long silence. At this juncture, a welcome diversion was supplied by the party bore, who interposed himself between Mike and Laura and plunged straight into a philosophical discussion about death. Laura seized her chance with alacrity. She walked off, leaving the two biggest bores in the room to fend for themselves.

She knew that if she was spotted by either Phil or Helen the game would be up and so decided to hide herself away in the bedroom until the party was over. Making a space on the bed among a pile of coats, she cuddled up with a book and was just beginning to congratulate herself on finding the perfect sanctuary when the door opened a fraction and she heard voices. Desperate measures were called for, and Laura resorted to play-acting. Propping herself up on one elbow, she talked urgently into the pile of coats.

'Mike, stop it – there's somebody coming.'

Whoever they were, the interlopers were suitably disconcerted, and they quickly stumbled out of the room. Pleased with her Oscar-winning performance, Laura smiled and then realized with some amazement that she had used Mike's name. She screwed up her face in distaste and then gave the coats a steamy, sexual look. In a voice husky with desire she played out a mock love scene.

'Oh, Mike, you magnificent animal!' she breathed into the lapel of a suitably dull tweed coat. 'Do you know what I want you to do now? I want you to undress me very slowly and whilst you're doing it I want . . . yes . . . I'll say it . . . I want you to drive me mad by talking about your bloody boring stone walls.'

This made her laugh out loud but, just as she was settling down to her book, she heard someone else approaching. Having warmed up nicely to her theme, she decided to go the whole hog. As if in the throes of some unbelievable multiple orgasm, she gasped Mike's name repeatedly and writhed around on the bed, clutching the tweed overcoat to her chest. After a flurry of sexual frenzy, she drew back lazily from the coat and opened her eyes to see Mike standing at the foot of the bed. Acute embarrassment made Laura lash out instinctively.

'Oh, look, are you following me about?'

'That's the last thing I'd do,' he said, staring strangely at her and the rumpled bed.

'Good.'

He turned to go, but his curiousity got the better of him. 'Why were you saying "Mike" like that?' he asked.

'Was I?' said Laura casually.

'Yes. "Oh, Mike! Mike!" you said.'

'If you must know, I was trying to keep people out.'

'Oh. I see.' Something was still obviously bothering him. 'Why "Mike", though?'

'Don't read anything into it.'

'Difficult not to.'

'It's just the first name that came into my head. I mean – tonight – what's the first girl's name that would come into *your* head?'

'Helen,' he said, without hesitation.

'Oh.' Typical.

'What are you doing here anyway?'

'Taking sanctuary.'

'Me too. I was going to get on with the crossword in the loo but somebody's in there.'

'Wait here if you like,' Laura said, feeling in a generous mood.

'Thanks.'

He sat gingerly on the edge of the bed, as far away from Laura as possible. She picked up her book and started to read again. At a loss for something to do,

Mike stretched out to pick up the alarm clock to check the time. It was intended to be a casual move, but in his awkwardness it seemed *too* casual. Laura made an ostentatious show of moving away which irritated Mike intensely.

'This is daft,' he said. 'We're hiding from each other and here we are on the same bed.'

Laura smiled faintly. 'It's no good going down, or we'll have Helen and Phil trying to glue us together again.'

'You get pretty hostile about that, don't you?'

'Don't *you*?'

'No. You can always live in hope, can't you? I mean, meeting women at my age – I don't know where they *are* any more. I even went to an Over-Twenty-Fives' Dance Night once, and I was the youngest one there. So, if I'm asked to, I come to parties. I hate parties but I come because sooner or later I might meet someone who's not just this real dog that everyone's trying to palm off on me.'

The words were out before it dawned on Mike that this telling definition had obviously included Laura. She glared at him.

'I'm sorry. I didn't mean . . .' he stuttered.

'You big-head!' she spat out. 'Why do you think *you* get invited? Do you think people have got Jane Fonda staying with them for the weekend and say, "Now who can we invite for Jane? I know – of course, Mike!" '

'If it was Jane Fonda I wouldn't mind!' Mike joked, trying to lighten the conversation a little.

'*She* would,' Laura said with feeling.

'Yes, but she can afford to be choosy.'

'And I can't?'

'I didn't say that. But be realistic. You're not as . . . you're hardly . . . well, you're older than Jane Fonda.'

This hurt. 'I'm not,' Laura snapped.

'Look, I don't know how she got into the conversation. I'm talking about ordinary people and all I'm saying – '

'I know what you're saying. How old are you – fifty?' she enquired spitefully.

'Forty-three.'

'Forty-three – you have about as much social grace as one of your bits of stone and you've got the bloody arrogance to expect to be fixed up with someone who isn't as dull as you.'

'What about you? What gives you the right to be so choosy?'

'Because I have the right!' Laura shouted. 'Just because I'm plain or homely or downright ugly doesn't mean that I have to jump at anything in trousers that bothers to say "Hello" to me.'

'That's what I meant. Substitute "skirt" for "trousers" and that's what I meant,' Mike explained.

Laura thought about this and reluctantly conceded that he might have a point. 'Oh. Yes, I see,' she said in a subdued voice.

Peace descended as they both retired hurt to their corners. The door swung open and Helen burst into the room. She was convinced that Laura was hiding away, but when she saw Mike sitting on the bed with her sister lolling on a pile of coats she stopped in mid-accusation. Realizing that he was in a compromising situation, Mike started to offer an explanation, but Laura cut in quickly.

'Come on, Helen – play the game,' she said meaningfully.

'Of course. Yes, of course,' Helen said. 'I had no idea. You carry on with what you were doing – talking about. You carry on.' As pleased as punch, she left the room, closing the door softly behind her.

Mike couldn't believe his ears. He rounded on

Laura. 'Now why did you give your sister the idea that we were in the bedroom together?'

'Well, we are.'

'Ah, yes, but it's hardly a romantic tryst though, is it? If the loo hadn't been occupied, I'd have been in there doing the crossword and you'd have been in here reading.'

'It's better for Helen to think she saw what she thought she saw,' Laura explained. 'It will make her whole evening.'

'She's very attractive, isn't she, Helen?' Mike said thoughtfully.

'Yes,' Laura hissed through clenched teeth. How much more of this artful flattery could one woman take in an evening?

Realizing he'd dropped yet another brick, Mike hastened to reassure her. 'And so are you,' he said dutifully.

'Oh, come on.'

'No, in your own way . . .'

His clumsy way with words was only making matters worse, and Mike decided to resort to some direct action instead. Believing that a quick kiss would put everything right, he grabbed the unsuspecting Laura by the shoulders. She collapsed backwards and yelled out as she cracked her head on the brass bead-stead. Simultaneously, Mike felt a sharp and sickening pain in his groin as he fell awkwardly on a sharp object under the pile of coats.

'You berk, that was my head,' Laura complained.

He apologized gruffly as he rooted around beneath the coats. Unearthing the deadly weapon – a leather briefcase – he hurled it across the room.

'Now why bring that to a party? And it would have poncey gold initials on it, wouldn't it?' he said bitterly. 'Are you all right?' he asked Laura, as an afterthought.

'Yes,' she said rubbing her head. 'What did you want to go and do that for?'

'Well, we don't seem to be meeting about anything else, and at least . . . touching . . . well, it gives you something to remember the day by, doesn't it? I mean, if I went to a party when I was a kid . . . well, at least I didn't feel it had been a total washout if I'd at least put my hand on a girl's knee.'

The sheer insensitivity and schoolboy prurience made Laura see red. She grabbed his hand and slapped it down over her left knee. 'There. Your evening has not been a total washout.'

Mike snatched his hand away. 'That is the single most unromantic act I've ever seen in my life.'

'Second only to your adolescent attempt to fracture my skull.'

'We're wasting our time, aren't we?' Mike said wearily.

'I think we are. Let's go.'

'Where?'

'Home.'

Mike started to mumble a polite excuse.

'I'm not inviting you to my home,' Laura said impatiently. 'I just want to go home but I think we'd best leave together.'

'Why?'

God, this man was dim. 'Because it's early and if either one of us tries to make it to the front door on his or her own . . .'

Light dawned. 'Yes,' agreed Mike, 'that makes sense. Did you have a coat?' he enquired, cheering up immensely at the thought of getting away at last.

'No,' she said flatly, 'just a briefcase' – and she retrieved it from the floor.

He had been made to look foolish so many times that evening that this latest *faux pas* scarcely registered with him.

'Do you have false teeth?' Laura asked unexpectedly.

'No,' Mike said indignantly. 'Why?'

'Because, when you kissed me, I heard this strange clicking sound.'

'Must have been one of the bones in my surgical corset.' It was the wittiest thing he had said all night, but it was said with considerable venom. He opened the door. They both put on suitably happy faces and headed for the front door.

After the Great Escape, they stood on the pavement in the cold night air and looked at each other bleakly.

'Well, we made it,' Laura said. 'Goodnight.' And she turned to walk away.

Relief made Mike generous. 'Let me give you a lift at least,' he offered.

Laura looked askance at his dilapidated van but decided that anything was better than walking. She shrugged. Mike slid open the passenger door and she climbed in. When she saw the passenger seat at close quarters, she baulked slightly. It consisted of a rickety wicker chair secured tenuously to the floor by bits of string. Gingerly she settled herself as best she could on the dusty seat. Mike slid the door shut and then walked round the front of the van. Laura watched dispassionately as he struggled to open the door on the driver's side, gave it up as a bad job, and trudged round the front of the van again. He opened the passenger door, clambered over her lap and eased himself into the driver's seat.

'Where to?' he asked.

'Fulham,' Laura said. 'Is it out of your way?'

'Yes,' Mike replied flatly. This didn't really surprise him – it was just the perfect end to a perfect evening, after all.

He started the van and they pulled away. Laura's chair tipped back, and she just managed to save herself from toppling backwards by making a quick grab for the door handle.

The journey was cold, miserable and silent. After what seemed like a lifetime, they arrived outside the block of flats where Laura lived. For a few moments they sat staring through the windscreen in a depressed trance.

'So,' Mike said.

'So.'

He looked at his watch. 'It's still only half past nine.'

'Doesn't time fly when you're having a rotten time?'

Mike forced a weak smile, then had a sudden thought. 'Look, what about a curry?' he asked.

'Ugh!' Something else they didn't have in common, she thought dismally. That figured.

'Chinese?' she countered.

'Hate it. Italian?'

'Where?'

'I don't know.' And he couldn't honestly be bothered to find out either. 'We're making noises, aren't we? Let's cut our losses.'

'Probably best,' Laura said as she started to climb out of the van.

'Goodbye, Mike.'

He made a half-hearted move to help, but she motioned him to stay where he was.

'Goodbye, Laura.'

He watched as she walked towards the block of flats. From a distance, she looked lonely and vulnerable, and he experienced a sudden pang of regret. Maybe one of them should have tried harder. Surely something could be salvaged out of the wreckage of the evening? As Laura reached the entrance to the flats, he jerked into action. He started to open the van door, but then remembered it was stuck. Hastily, he clambered over the wicker chair and jumped out on the other side. He raced up to the building but, by the time he reached the lobby, Laura had disappeared from view and the automatic doors were locked against him. Quickly, he scanned the rows of name-plates but foolishly recalled that he didn't even know her name. Oh well, at least he'd given it a whirl. He shrugged and walked slowly back to his van. Unthinkingly, he tried to open the driver's door – it slid back effortlessly.

'Yes, you would open now, wouldn't you? You just would,' Mike snarled. He climbed in and slammed the door behind him. As he drove away, defeated, into the night, the handle fell off and landed with a dull clank in the gutter.

2

By one of those strange little ironies of life, usually monopolized by only the best Victorian novelists, Mike and Laura were shortly to be reunited on the very scene of their first memorable meeting. As fate would have it, Phil and Helen were the unwitting stooges in the farcical series of events, but it should be said that, if it hadn't been for Laura's stupid pride and Mike's innate unimaginativeness, the whole affair would have ended conclusively on Saturday night outside Laura's flat.

When Helen phoned mid-morning to invite her sister to lunch, Laura rashly decided to imply that not only had she and Mike hit it off at the party but had also hit it off to the extent of spending the night locked in each other's arms. Delighted that her sister should at last have made a conquest, Helen pressed for further details when Laura arrived at her flat, but Laura became strangely evasive about the subject, leaving Helen's imagination to work overtime.

Meanwhile, down at the pub, Mike, who had run into Phil, was telling a slightly different story.

'Give you the elbow, did she?' Phil asked in his disarmingly straightforward way.

'No. Elbows were not involved. It was mutual consent on the grounds of mutual antipathy.'

'Well, you can't win them all, can you?'

Mike, who had during the course of his forty-three years in the world won very few, merely nodded.

Noticing that his friend was looking a bit down in

23

the mouth, and feeling rather sorry for him, Phil invited him home for lunch. The choice between Helen's cooking and the day-old spam fritters mouldering away at his flat was not a difficult one for Mike to make, and he left the pub in slighly higher spirits than when he had entered.

Four very mixed-up people, therefore, came face to face in the middle of Phil and Helen's living-room: Helen was delighted to see her sister's lover; Phil was embarrassed; Mike immediately suspected a double-cross; while Laura at least had the decency to blush. Blithely unaware of the various and deep emotional undercurrents, Helen dragged Phil off to the kitchen, leaving the happy couple alone with each other.

The kitchen door had barely closed before Laura pounced. 'Why did you have to turn up here?' she hissed.

'Why did *you* have to turn up here?' retaliated Mike, who saw his nice uncomplicated Sunday lunch receding and several hours of embarrassment stretching ahead.

'I was invited.'

'Oh, fine, because I gatecrashed,' Mike said, resenting intensely the tone in Laura's voice. 'I happened to be passing and I thought, "How about inviting myself to lunch?" So I did.'

'Couldn't you go somewhere else?'

If Mike had been a violent man he would have hit her.

'You're all warmth you, aren't you?' he said bitterly.

Laura suddenly caught sight of her sister eavesdropping round the kitchen door. Realizing she had a romantic role to sustain, she smiled warmly at Mike.

'Honestly, Mike, I couldn't think of a nicer surprise than you turning up like this,' she purred.

Helen returned to the kitchen, smiling smugly.

Mike edged away. 'Are you having some form of treatment?' he asked warily.

'There's no need to upset them, is there?'

'I'm not upsetting anyone. I'm sitting here talking to a schizophrenic.'

'Well, if you went away, you wouldn't have to, would you?'

At this point, Phil, obviously egged on by Helen, decided to take a quick check on the proceedings. Laura immediately spotted his grin and changed tack once more.

'I was thinking of calling you today, anyway,' she murmured endearingly as she snuggled up to Mike.

Looking confused, Phil popped back into the kitchen to confer with Helen.

'What were you going to call me on – your little red plastic telephone with the magic bell?' Mike asked sarcastically.

'They keep looking,' Laura explained.

'Oh. You're being watched as well.' This woman had all the classic symptoms.

'You know who I mean – Phil and Helen. Look, they think we left the party early last night because we were getting very' – she cast around for the right word – 'friendly.'

'I know,' said Mike, who was still confused.

'And they don't know any different.'

'Phil does.'

'How?' Laura looked at him beadily.

'I told him.'

'You did what?'

'Well, he asked.'

'You bloody back-stabber,' Laura snarled. She flounced over to the window and stared moodily into the distance.

Mike, who was an uncomplicated fellow at heart,

tried to make some sense of the convoluted reasoning behind this accusation.

'There's a cherry tree in the garden,' Laura announced. 'Why don't you go and chop it down?'

'What for?'

'So that when somebody says "Who chopped that cherry tree down?" you can say, "I did. I, George Washington, did." '

'I'm getting fed up with you! All I do is tell the plain facts of the matter and — ' A sudden thought occurred. 'Just a minute, why should that bother you unless you've made up a different version?'

Laura made a brave stab at a light and dismissive laugh but missed by a mile.

'You have. You must have,' Mike said triumphantly.

Now any other woman would have realized that the game was up, but not Laura. Even if she were going down with the *Titanic*, she would have pretended it was a submarine.

'Well, what I actually did was go along with an assumption which Helen made. I knew that your ego would never allow you to admit that you didn't even get through my front door.'

It seemed a plausible enough reason to Laura, but Mike wasn't going to swallow this. 'You didn't know I'd be here to say anything at all,' he pointed out.

'Ah!' she said, playing for time.

'Yes, "Ah!", ' Mike said, warning now to his theme. 'Now, according to popular fiction, it's men who are supposed to boast of conquests they've never made. It's us who are supposed to stick little flags on the side of our cockpits.'

'A singularly apt phrase,' Laura noted wryly.

'A singularly apt phrase,' echoed Mike, who was now beginning to pace up and down like the prosecuting counsel at a murder trial. 'So why have you done it?'

A slow weariness began to creep over Laura. Perhaps the time had come to admit defeat. 'All right, if you must know, perhaps I'm sick of *not* being the flag on somebody's cockpit,' she said, deliberately avoiding Mike's gaze. 'Happy?'

'No. Sad,' he said, and looked more keenly at her. For the first time in their short and tempestuous relationship it seemed they had something in common after all.

Feeling herself close to tears, Laura went on the attack again. 'Now don't you start feeling sorry for me.'

'I just feel sorry that anybody should have to do that,' Mike said quietly, 'and I know what I'm talking about because I've done it myself. I've lied.'

'So why pick this time to tell the truth?'

'I don't know. Perhaps I felt a finer type of person this morning. Perhaps I was actually concerned about your honour.'

'Oh, cobblers to my honour!' Laura snapped. 'What about my pride?'

Mike had always tended to believe in the old-fashioned virtues of life, and Laura's reaction came as something of a shock.

Helen bustled into the room. 'Lunch is ready,' she announced gaily.

It was after lunch that matters became marginally more complicated. Separately and unknown to each other, the two protagonists decided to change their stories. In a last-ditch effort to save Laura's pride, Mike lied to Phil, while Laura came clean with Helen and told the truth. Shortly after these revelations, Mike and Laura wisely decided to make a tactical retreat to the pub, leaving behind a very confused couple indeed.

For the lonely and unloved of this world, there's something about Sundays that feeds their hopelessness. Sunday afternoons, in particular, have a depressing quality all of their own. On Fridays there's always hope of the unexpected – the chance meeting, an invitation to a party. Saturdays are usually spent in happy expectation of a night out. After the party, there's only Sunday left, and Sundays have a tendency to hang around like a defeating mist. The evening stretches ahead with only Monday to look forward to.

Laura's 'highspot' of the day was doing the ironing and watching *Songs of Praise*, while Mike relied upon warmed-up spam fritters to deaden the pain. After leaving the pub, they stuck desperately together and, when Mike ventured to invite Laura out for dinner, she decided to postpone the ironing.

The restaurant was one of those pretentious little bistros that seem to proliferate in the newly fashionable suburbs of Chelsea. Mike clambered out of his van and tried to penetrate the interior by peering through the steamed-up window.

'What are you doing?' shouted Laura from her precarious perch on the wicker chair.

'Trying to see if it's full.'

'Wouldn't it be easier to go in and ask?' Laura suggested with that straightforward female logic that seems to infuriate most men.

'No. You feel such a fool if you have to walk out again.'

'Well, is it full or not?' Laura demanded testily.

'I can't see. The windows are steamed up.'

At this moment a man inside the restaurant rubbed a circle in the misted glass and looked out. Mike took a step backwards in confusion.

'What's the matter?' Laura yelled.

'A face just looked out.'

'Well, we know *somebody*'s in there.'

'I'll ask.'

Mike tapped on the glass. The face stared at him through the circle and Mike deliberately mouthed at it, 'Is it full in there? Are all the tables taken?'

The face looked blank.

'I said,' continued Mike doggedly, 'is it full in there?'

Laura decided that, if they were to get something to eat before the restaurant closed, she would have to take matters into her own hands and, unseen by Mike, she walked calmly inside.

Meanwhile, the pavement pantomime continued.

'Can you rub a bigger circle so I can see?'

The owner of the face decided to give a little wave to placate this gastronomic voyeur.

'No,' said Mike, mouthing more deliberately. 'Watch my lips!'

Another circle, alongside the original one, appeared and Mike found himself staring at a vaguely familiar face. The face belonged to Laura and she was beckoning him inside. Slightly annoyed, but with as much dignity as he could muster, Mike entered the restaurant. The first thing that struck him was that there were plenty of empty tables.

'It's no good going by empty tables,' he said defensively. 'They could all be reserved.'

'I played it clever,' Laura said sardonically. 'I asked.'

Mike recognized the man behind the face sitting at a table near the window. Feeling that some kind of explanation was in order, he started to apologize but was thrown somewhat when the man replied in French. He struggled to remember some appropriate French phrase but couldn't get further than '*Je m'excuse*' and 'um'.

Realizing that this multilingual interchange was leading nowhere fast, Laura cut it short. '*Il faut excuser mon ami, monsieur, mais il est complètement fou,*' she rattled off in faultless style.

'*Ah! Quel dommage!*' The Frenchman smiled at her sympathetically.

As they arranged themselves on the uncomfortably low banquette in the cocktail bar, Mike seemed to be puzzling over something. Then realization dawned. '*Fou . . . fou . . .* that means crackers! You told him I was crackers!' he said indignantly.

'Well, if you'd been sitting where he was sitting, looking at you through the window . . .'

'Still . . .'

The waiter arrived and asked if they would like to order drinks. There was some initial confusion over this because, rather to Mike's annoyance, Laura insisted on ordering for herself. Consequently, they both ended up speaking in awkward unison. Mike was not exactly a bon viveur and generally felt out of his depth in restaurants. It seemed that, the more he tried to appear self-assured and relaxed, the more mistakes he made.

A waiter swept past with a covered folder under his arm.

'I'll take that, thank you,' Mike said, reaching out and handing what he thought was the menu to Laura. 'There you are. Now what would you like to eat?'

She handed it back to him. 'It's the wine list.'

Mike sighed in resignation.

'You don't have to try and impress me, you know,' she said gently.

'I'm not, that's the trouble. When I *try* to be impressive it really goes to pieces.'

It was an uncomfortable start to the evening, and matters didn't improve. While she was reading the menu, Laura dropped the bombshell.

'I've lost a contact lens.'

'Here?'

'It must be here. It was in a minute ago.'

'Well, where is it?'

'Why do people always ask that when you lose something?' she said irritably. Then she yanked at the collar of her dress and stared intently at her bra.

'What's going on?' Mike asked warily.

'They sometimes drop down your clothing.'

In an effort to appear helpful, Mike leant over and peered inside Laura's dress with her. She jerked herself away.

'What on earth do you think you're doing?'

'Looking for your contact lens.'

'I'll look down there if it's all the same to you.' And she continued with her intimate investigation.

Aware of the curious glances of other customers and the raised eyebrows of the maître d', Mike did his best to smile unconcernedly.

'Are you wearing anything that would stop it falling straight through?' he enquired cautiously.

'What kind of question is that?'

'I'm just trying to help. Look, wiggle about a bit and I'll look on the floor.' In for a penny, in for a pound.

As unobtrusively as possible, Laura gyrated on the spot, while Mike got down on his hands and knees and studied the floor. Somehow the meticulous search spread like wildfire, and for ten minutes business ground to a halt as Mike and Laura tried to prevent customers from treading on the invisible and precious lens. In Mike's opinion, the maître d' became unnecessarily testy when he asked if the cocktail bar could be cordoned off for a while. Eventually, however, the search paid off. The lens was located and Mike and Laura resumed their seats, dishevelled but relieved.

'Thanks ever so much,' Laura said. 'I wouldn't have had the nerve to do all that if you hadn't been there.'

'Well, some men impress women by stopping runaway horses. I find contact lenses,' Mike quipped, relieved to find that he had contributed something to the evening.

They both became aware that the maître d' was looming over them and the raised eyebrows were very much in evidence.

'Ah, jolly good. I think we're ready to order now,' Mike said with an authority and confidence he did not feel.

The eyebrows quivered disdainfully.

Hungry and tired, the bon viveurs found themselves at Laura's flat toying with an indifferent take-away which was congealing before their eyes. Apart from the unappetizing smell, there was a definite atmosphere in the air.

'They're quite good really, aren't they, these take-aways?' Mike said stoically.

A sullen silence greeted this statement.

'Quite good. Quite good value too,' Mike said as he watched Laura push her plate deliberately aside. 'All right, so we got slung out of a restaurant! What's so awful about that?'

'Because we wanted to eat there, that's why!'

'Look, it wasn't *my* contact lens that started it all. Why you don't just wear glasses – '

'I don't like wearing glasses.'

'That's vanity.'

This was the standard male jibe about women refusing to wear glasses, and Laura was sick to death of hearing it. 'I know what it is,' she snapped.

'You'd look more attractive wearing glasses than crawling about on the floor looking for a contact lens.'

'I've known men who like women crawling about on the floor.'

'In restaurants?' Mike asked incredulously.

'Well – no.'

'There you are then. Next time wear your glasses.'

'What next time?'

He wasn't going to be caught out like this. He wasn't going to feed her the line she obviously wanted. 'The next time somebody takes you out to dinner.'

'Oh. Well, the next time you take somebody out to dinner and you're asked to leave, try standing up for yourself.'

'You saw the size of that waiter.'

'I'm not talking about fighting. I'm talking about . . . about . . .'

Mike completed the sentence for her. 'Somebody else.'

'Yes.'

There was a hostile silence.

'Coffee?' Laura asked in a tone of voice that defied acceptance.

'No, thanks.'

She was hoping that he would take the hint and go. They'd only known each other for forty-eight hours but it seemed like forty-eight weeks. Mike sat stolidly at the table. The Special Fried Rice had set like quick-mix concrete and he nudged it around his plate. He'd wanted everything to work out. He'd wanted to impress her and to be able to relax with her but somehow everything seemed to have conspired against him. Laura disappeared into the kitchen and Mike tried another mouthful of food. It made him feel nauseous and he pushed his plate away. Laura returned with an ironing-board under her arm and he looked on in disbelief as she set up the board and plugged in an iron.

'You certainly know how to entertain a bloke,' he said bitterly.

'What did you expect, a strip-tease?'

'I wouldn't mind.'

'I've got to do it. I'm going to Brussels tomorrow,' Laura explained matter-of-factly.

'Holiday?' Mike enquired politely.

'No. Work. There's a conference and a friend of mine got me in as an interpreter.'

'How long will you be gone?'

'Oh, about a week.'

'Um ... I couldn't have seen you next week, anyway, because I'm going to be very busy myself.'

They both knew what the other meant. They were politely telling each other to get lost.

'Well, if you're not going to do that strip-tease,' Mike said, getting up from the table.

'Some other time.'

'Yes. I'll phone you,' he said without conviction.

'Yes. I'll phone you,' she replied, not to be outdone in the rejection stakes.

'Watch the contact lenses.'

'We don't even know how to say goodbye,' Laura said sadly.

'I do,' he contradicted. Determined to get something right, he leant across the ironing-board and with one hand pulled a strangely compliant Laura towards him. As he moved in for a tender and memorable goodbye kiss, he inadvertently rested his free hand on the hot iron.

'Oh, Gordon bloody Bennett!' he shrieked and jumped back several yards.

'Are you all right?' Laura asked in some concern, feeling partly responsible for the accident.

'I'm fine. I'm fine. The perfect end to the perfect

34

day,' Mike said through clenched teeth. 'Goodbye, Laura,' he said stiffly, and walked towards the door.

'Goodbye, Mike,' Laura said, and watched him leave. She stood looking at the closed door for several minutes, then she shook her head and returned half-heartedly to her ironing. What else was there left?

It was while she was working at the conference in Brussels that Laura met Ben. After the unnerving and confidence-crushing interlude with Mike, Ben was the perfect antidote: he was handsome, self-assured, tall and, above all, romantic. Ben certainly knew how to treat a woman, and Laura couldn't believe her luck when arrangements were made to continue the liaison in London.

In a rash mood, she invited Ben to her flat for a small dinner party. It had to be a *small* dinner party because cooking was not exactly Laura's forte and, if she had to cater for more than four guests, things were apt to go wrong on a grand scale. Wisely, therefore, she restricted the guest list to three – Phil, Helen and, of course, the delectable Ben, whom she fully intended to flaunt in her sister's face.

Helen and Phil were the first to arrive. Laura was in an obvious state of advanced anxiety. Pausing only to hand out drinks, she rushed back into the kitchen from whence could be heard the hysterical banging of many pots and pans and the occasional culinary expletive. While Helen fiddled about with the table arrangements, Phil sat back and nursed his drink. There was a rather wistful, faraway look in her husband's eyes, and Helen enquired if he were hungry.

'I would be if *you* were cooking the dinner,' he said ruefully.

'Now that's not fair. Laura's a very good cook on her day.'

'I must have missed it.'

A flustered chef emerged from the kitchen. 'Well, that's done it! My Floating Islands have sunk!' she announced dramatically.

'What Floating Islands?' asked Phil, greatly intrigued by this unexpected geographical catastrophe.

'Pudding,' Laura explained. 'Special custard with little floating islands of meringue. Only they're not floating. They've sunk.'

'They'll taste the same,' said Phil, who was practical but rather dense when it came to the finer points of food presentation.

'That's not the point. They float in the picture in the book, but do they float for me? No.'

'All right, calm down. I'll have a look,' Helen volunteered.

'Would you?' Laura asked in some relief.

'Just relax. Sit down. Talk to Phil and relax.'

While Helen went to survey the islands, Laura sat on the edge of the sofa next to Phil. In between sips of her medicinal sherry, she kept sneaking glances at her watch.

'I'd hate to see you when you're tense,' he remarked.

'I know. Silly, isn't it?' She looked at her watch again.

'This Ben, does he have this effect on you all the time?'

' 'Fraid so.'

'Hmmmmmm.'

With eyes like gimlets she turned and looked at him. 'What's that supposed to mean?'

'You wouldn't be in this state if Mike were coming to dinner.'

36

'You make that sound like an accusation – and, no, I wouldn't.'

For some reason, she felt rather guilty and added apologetically, 'I like him, Phil, but he's not the sort of man to get me into any state at all.'

'Not even drunk.'

'He never tried that.'

'Well, I'm afraid you've had the floating bit,' said Helen, returning from the scene of the disaster, 'but we'll sling in some peaches, soak it in brandy, set light to it and call it Flaming Islands instead.'

'The last time I flambéd anything, I burned off my left eyebrow,' Laura said doubtfully.

'I'll flambé. You take the credit.'

'Sounds fair.' Laura looked at her watch for the hundredth time. 'Ben should be here soon.'

'This is beginning to sound like the Second Coming,' Phil joked.

'You'll like him. Everybody does.'

'He's not one of these Life and Soul of the Party jokers, is he?' Phil asked suspiciously.

'What *is* the matter with you?' Helen said, giving him a warning look.

'He thinks it should be Mike,' Laura said.

'I just think he's a nice chap,' Phil said defensively.

'I'm not old enough to settle for nice. When I get the blue rinse, then I might settle for nice.'

Phil turned to his wife. 'Do you know what she means by that?'

'Yes,' she smiled.

'Oh. Well, if I was a woman, I'd rate niceness very high.'

'With your legs you'd have to,' Helen pointed out.

'I wouldn't have my legs if I were a woman, would I? They wouldn't be thin and hairy. No, they'd be long and slender – rather lovely.' And he smiled at this pulchritudinous vision.

'We don't choose our own equipment, you know,' Laura said tersely. 'We're stuck with what we get.'

'Now look what you've started,' Helen said, realizing they were on very dodgy ground as far as Laura was concerned.

'No, it's all right,' Laura interceded. 'I am not going to lose my temper with this slender-legged lovely, because I am not in a temper-losing mood. Honestly, Phil, when you meet Ben you'll see what I mean. He's . . .' She paused, not wishing to become a bore on the subject. 'Let's just say I'm very lucky.'

The telephone rang and Laura rushed over to answer it.

'Hello? Ben? Where are you? Oh. But you're supposed to – ' Phil and Helen exchanged knowing glances. 'Why? Your *what*?' An iciness crept into Laura's voice. 'No, you didn't ever mention it. Well, do give her my very best, won't you? No, I don't want to talk. I'm going to hang up now because I don't approve of obscene telephone calls and, if I say anything else, this is going to become one.'

She slammed down the receiver, marched over to the drinks table and poured herself a very stiff drink. Aware that Phil and Helen were looking rather concernedly at her, she said in a falsely bright voice:

'And there's another thing about Ben. He's full of surprises – like being married.'

And so the carefully planned dinner party became slightly more intimate than Laura had anticipated. Her guests decided it would be more diplomatic in the circumstances to leave, and Laura sat down at the dinner table in sombre solitude. She had another drink, quickly followed by a second. For some reason she couldn't bring herself to get up and clear away the table and wondered idly if she would end up like

Miss Haversham in *Great Expectations*. Perhaps when Phil and Helen called round at some time in the future, they would still find her dressed up in all her finery, with cobwebs and dust covering the perfectly laid silver and china. Resolving to do *something*, she suddenly remembered the pudding and went into the kitchen. Following her sister's rescue plan, she poured half a bottle of brandy over the sunken islands, but without Helen's expertise she decided to forgo the flambé part – anyway it was a waste of good brandy. Rather unsteadily, she carried the bowl of 90 per cent proof custard back to the table and began tucking in with a grim determination. She thought of her last evening in Brussels with Ben and then she thought of him cosily at home with his wife. Feeling lonely and sorry for herself, she started to cry. Tears trickled down her face and plopped on to the disintegrating remains of the sunken islands. The doorbell rang, and she weaved across the room to answer it. Mike was standing nervously on the doorstep. Laura looked at him blearily.

'Hello, I was passing,' he lied.

'Are you nice?' she slurred, propping herself up carefully against the wall.

'What? I don't know. Who am I to judge?' Mike said modestly.

'You probably are.'

Taking this as an invitation, he made as if to step inside.

'So go away,' Laura said and pushed the door shut in his face. Mike was nice and straightforward, she decided – too nice and straightforward to find out about the sordid Ben affair.

Realizing that all was far from well, Mike chose to ignore this rebuff and, pushing the door open, he followed her into the living room.

'You've been crying,' he said accusingly.

39

'I have not.'

'What's that water running down your cheek?'

'I'm leaking,' she said, and sat down abruptly at the table. Carefully Laura refilled her empty glass. 'Don't you take this glass away,' she said warningly, as she saw Mike's hand reach out.

'I wasn't going to. I'd like one myself.'

'Oh. That's all right then.'

Mike poured himself a drink and sat opposite her. 'Would you like some Floating Flaming Sunken Drunken Islands?' she asked.

He looked at the rather doubtful contents of the bowl and politely declined.

'Very wise,' Laura congratulated him.

'What's the matter?' he asked.

'Nothing.'

'I'll put it another way. What's the matter?'

'What's the matter with *you*? There must be something the matter with you to make you keep asking what's the matter with *me*. "What's the matter? What's the matter?" What do you want to know for. Why should you care?'

'If you must know, I'm after my Rover Scouts Caring Badge. I listen to six people's problems and I get the badge. I've done five and you're all I've got left.'

She looked at him with her head on one side. In her inebriated state she was almost ready to go along with this idea.

'Anyway,' he persisted, 'I don't like nice people crying and I think you're a nice person.'

'If I knew how to do a hollow laugh, I'd do one.'

'Look, there's no need to feel guilty,' Mike said gently.

Laura jumped. 'Guilty! I . . . guilty about what?'

'About not phoning me when you got back from Brussels. I didn't phone you either.'

'Oh, that. Well, you see, there was a reason I didn't phone you. His name is Ben and I met him in Brussels.'

'Oh. So why have you been crying?'

'Nothing much. I just found out he's married.'

'You met him in Brussels and you've only just found out?'

'Yes.'

'What a prune!'

'I'd use stronger language than that to describe him.'

'Not him. You.'

'Oh. Well, thanks a lot! Thanks for being so sympathetic!' She turned her attention to the pudding and aggressively slurped up another spoonful.

'I do wish you'd stop stuffing that goo down you.'

'I like it,' she said defiantly.

'You're eating it because you're upset.'

'I'm eating it because it's lovely.'

'Surely it came up in the conversation,' Mike said, returning to the subject of Ben.

Laura experienced a slight but unmistakable queasiness. 'Don't say "came up",' she begged.

'Marriage,' he qualified.

'Well, it obviously didn't. Or I asked the question and developed hysterical deafness when he answered.'

'It's not as if you're a young girl,' he pointed out. Mr Diplomacy in person.

'Have you been to charm school while I was away?'

'None so blind as those who won't see, I suppose,' Mike continued, elaborating on his theme.

'Shut up!' Laura shouted.

'He must have seen you coming.'

'Shut up and go away! Leave me alone!'

The floodgates opened and Laura burst into tears. Mike got up from the table and, putting his arm around her, tried to move her gently towards the sofa.

'Get off me! Get off me!' She shrugged him away like a petulant child who wants to be comforted but who needs more coaxing. He kept a firm hold of her and managed to sit her down. Giving in with some considerable relief, Laura sobbed her heart out on his shoulder. Suddenly she felt the sunken islands begin to rise.

'Oh God, now I'm going to be sick!' she gasped.

'That's the first sensible thing you've said since I arrived,' Mike said as he steered her quickly towards the bathroom.

After that abortive dinner party, Laura never could bring herself to look custard in the face again, but, although Mike had witnessed her sordid downfall, she felt strangely grateful towards him – he had been around at the right time and provided some essential comfort. Mike discovered that he rather enjoyed being protective towards Laura, even though she had been the worse for drink at the time, and so they continued to see each other over the next few weeks and he became a regular visitor to Laura's flat.

Having survived a couple of major crises along the way, the relationship between them seemed to have strengthened considerably, but there was one major hurdle looming ahead and, the longer they put it off, the larger and more formidable it became.

Things came to a head when they were watching an old American movie on television late one evening. The film was the Bette Davies and Paul Henreid classic *Now Voyager*, and Laura was lapping it up. Mike, on the other hand, was finding it all rather tedious and stifled a yawn. Sensing, however, that the film had lulled Laura into a romantic mood, he thought he could take advantage of the situation. Perhaps a tender little kiss on the back of her neck might not come amiss – and he edged along the couch to the unsuspecting Laura, who was now leaning forward in an effort not to miss one single word of the plot. Aware only that Mike had fidgeted at a climactic moment in the film, Laura gestured impatiently at him to keep still. Stifling another yawn, he sat back and waited for the film to end, then, as the lushly sentimental music soared over the closing credits, he leant forward to plant the long-awaited kiss. Without warning, Laura sat back suddenly, banging her head sharply on Mike's chin. Both cried out in a mixture of pain and surprise.

'You could have had my front teeth out then!' Mike exclaimed, clutching his jaw.

'What about my head? What were you doing round there anyway?'

'I was going to kiss the back of your neck.' It all sounded rather silly now.

Laura got up and switched off the television set. 'Why?'

'Does there have to be a why? I felt like it.'

'Well, you should have waited till the film was over,' she said, rather ungraciously, Mike thought.

'Talk about pouring cold water on a romantic mood.'

'I had a romantic mood! I had Paul Henreid.'

'It didn't even have a happy ending,' Mike pointed out sullenly.

'It wasn't supposed to be happy – that's why it was so romantic.'

'Well, if your idea of romance is watching Paul Henreid sticking two fags in his mouth . . .'

'All right, clever. What's yours?'

Without hesitation Mike said: 'Barbarella. Jane Fonda peeling off that space suit.'

'Huh!'

'What do you mean, "Huh"?'

'That's not romance,' she scoffed. 'There wasn't even anybody else there.'

Mike smiled an annoyingly secretive smile. 'There was when I think about it.'

'It's just fantasy time with you, isn't it?'

'Are you telling me that as you, or as Bette Davies?'

Laura thought he might have a point there, but she was in a bad mood now and wasn't going to admit it. 'Anyway, it's all make-believe. It's all so perfect on there.'

Mike said, 'What about real life?'

'Ah, real life. Now that's different.'

'Isn't it, though? It's *us* in real life.'

'Us,' she repeated thoughtfully.

This was a distinctly sobering idea, and neither could bring themselves to look each other in the face. Mike knew that, as Laura seemed to have cast him as the Paul Henreid character in this romantic scene, he ought to make his move. He drew a deep breath and stood up.

'Well, shall I move the van, or what?' he asked.

'What are you talking about moving the van for?'

'Because it's parked outside and it's on a double yellow line,' he explained.

'You're all right. It's half past ten at night,' Laura said, looking at her watch.

'I know,' Mike said gruffly, 'but those traffic wardens – they're up at the crack of dawn, aren't they?' He shuffled his feet.

Then it hit her. 'My God, it *is* real life, isn't it? You're trying to seduce me and the first thing you think about is getting a parking ticket.'

'I'm not trying to seduce you. I just think it's time we slept together.' This all came out in a rush and Mike realized it didn't sound quite right, but at least it was out in the open at last.

'Oh,' she said, taken aback. Whatever she thought

of the proposal, she could scarcely accuse Mike of evasiveness.

'Well, it is, isn't it? It's been in the air for weeks now – like thunder.' Perhaps not the best simile to use in the circumstances, he thought, but then again. . . .

'Well, yes, I suppose it has,' Laura said.

'So do I move the van or what?'

'Will you shut up about your bloody van!' she snapped.

'All right! I'll leave it where it is and get a ticket in the morning. I won't mention it again. If that's your idea of romance, fine. I'll just get the ticket.'

Laura gave him a long, hard look, then picked up her handbag, took out six pounds and slapped the notes into Mike's hand.

'Well, that's a bit cold-blooded,' he said, feeling like a bought man. He put the money down hastily.

'Cold-blooded, that's rich!'

'Well, you're not making it any easier, are you?'

'What do you expect me to do?' Laura asked wearily.

'I don't know.'

They were feeling increasingly more awkward now – there had been too much debate beforehand and Mike felt that somewhere along the line he should have been more spontaneous and romantic. Bloody Paul Henreid.

'You do something,' Laura suggested.

'A pointer, really. I suppose I'm looking for a pointer,' he said desperately, looking round the room as though the answer might lie hidden there.

'Mike, that's really up to you,' Laura said quietly but firmly.

'Quite right.'

Seeming to resolve something, he stood up. Laura waited expectantly. Instead of moving towards her, however, he walked purposefully towards the front door.

'Where are you going?' she asked in amazement.

'To move the van off the double yellow lines.'

Exasperated beyond belief, she watched him go.

In an effort to save further embarrassment and delays, Laura decided to get ready for bed while Mike was safely out of the way. Hastily she undressed and then remembered that her best nightdress was in the wash, so she had to settle for the pink winceyette pyjamas. Carefully, she arranged herself on the couch and practised a few appealing poses. Time passed. It crossed her mind that Mike had lost his nerve altogether and had driven off into the night. Feeling chilly, she put on her dressing gown and snuggled up on the couch.

She must have dozed off because the next thing she heard was the doorbell ringing. Sleepily she got up to answer it. A dishevelled Mike was standing on the doorstep.

'Where did you park the van – Birmingham?'

'Sorry. I can't get it started. I wondered if you'd help me push it round the corner.'

'You have five seconds to rephrase that,' Laura said, preparing to slam the door in his face.

After an obvious mental struggle, Mike walked into the flat. 'Oh, blow the fine!' he said.

Laura slumped down on the sofa.

'No. I didn't mean it to sound like that,' he said quickly.

'Everything you say in this kind of situation sounds like that!'

'Well, hard luck! I'm not Paul Whatsisname!' Mike snapped.

'Henreid.'

'Him. But if that's what you want. Got any cigarettes?'

'There's some in the box. Why?' she asked.

He didn't answer but instead took two cigarettes from the box on the table and picked up a lighter. With some difficulty, he lit both cigarettes and then handed one to Laura.

'I don't smoke,' she said.

'Neither do I,' Mike admitted.

They looked at each other, but at least the ice was broken and the humour of the situation got to them both.

'We won't do that bit,' Laura said, smiling.

'Perhaps not,' agreed Mike, as he stubbed out the cigarettes in the ashtray.

The formalities were over. He helped Laura gently to her feet and, glancing over her shoulder, was riveted by the sight of the bedroom door. It was slightly ajar and all it lacked was a flashing neon sign. Laura swallowed nervously. Mike cleared his throat a couple of times. They both felt extremely weak at the knees and simultaneously sank down on the couch again. Looking down, Mike noticed Laura's pink winceyette pyjama legs with some disappointment.

'I've got a nightie, but it's in the wash,' Laura said awkwardly, trying to tuck the offending legs up under her dressing-gown.

'No, they're fine. They're very' – he cast around for the right compliment – 'very dinky.'

This uninspired description did not exactly fill Laura with any confidence. 'Dinky?' she said in distaste.

'It's not my day for words, is it?'

He looked so dejected that Laura wanted to take him in her arms and cuddle him. 'It doesn't matter, Mike,' she said gently.

'It does. I'd like to say something now that was just right.'

'Why?'

'Because you'd like me to.'

'Look, if you can get by without the sheer black nightie, I can get by without the words,' Laura said, and leant forward for a kiss.

Quickly looking around to ensure that there were no pain-producing objects about, Mike leaned towards her. They kissed softly, only their lips touching.

'Neither of us got hurt,' Laura said quietly.

'Good sign,' Mike said, much encouraged.

She started to help him out of his jacket. It was an awkward manoeuvre to perform from a sitting-down position and, although one arm slipped out easily, the lining of the other sleeve was torn and it pulled inside out, trapping Mike's arm inside. Giving an extra strong tug, Laura succeeded in twisting the arm round at a painful angle. He yelled out in pain and jerked away, causing the lining to rip even further.

Laura started to apologize.

'Never mind,' he said, 'It was only an old jacket.' As if to prove his point he threw it on the floor. As luck would have it, his aim was bad – Mike missed the floor and the jacket skidded over the top of the coffee table, knocking off several ornaments.

Mike stood up immediately to clear up the mess, but Laura prevented him by taking off her dressing-gown and flinging it over the debris.

'Leave it till morning,' she said. 'We've got to get up early anyway.'

'Why?'

'To push the van off those double yellow lines,' she smiled.

48

Mike smiled back and, taking her hand, led her into the bedroom.

The earth did not move.

3

Laura was hunched over her desk, busy translating the manuscript of a novel. It was turgid stuff and she was quite relieved when an interruption was provided by the arrival of her sister.

'I can't stop,' Helen said breathlessly the moment she stepped inside the living-room.

'Oh. All right. Nice to have seen you. Ta-ta.'

'For long, I mean.' Helen took off her coat and, just as she was about to settle herself down, noticed the work scattered over Laura's desk.

'Oh, you're working,' she apologized.

'No, any excuse to leave that,' Laura said.

'What is it?'

'A novel.'

'A novel? You told me that a novel is a translator's dream.'

'Not this one. It's about a man who loses his soul in a plastics factory.'

'Does he find it again?' asked Helen.

'I haven't got that far. He's still agonizing at the moment – he's been agonizing for the last eighty pages.'

Laura joined Helen on the couch. 'Well, cheer up. Phil and I thought we'd eat out tonight. What about you and Mike coming?'

'Um . . . no,' Laura said slowly, 'I don't think so. Coffee?'

Helen wasn't going to be sidetracked like this. 'No thanks. Why not?'

'Well, I don't exactly know what Mike is doing this evening,' Laura said, hoping that Helen would swallow the excuse without further discussion.

'Ask him.'

'I might not be able to. A glass of wine?' she offered, getting up from the couch abruptly.

'No, thanks. Look, would you like me to write out an invitation and you can just hand it to him?'

'No, well, actually I don't know if I'll be seeing Mike tonight. I haven't seen him for two or three days,' Laura admitted.

'You haven't had a row?' Helen asked in some concern.

'No. It's just that from time to time I don't see him. He – well, he sort of goes walkabout,' she finished lamely, and sat down again.

'Like an aborigine?' Helen grinned.

'Yes. He doesn't carry a spear but it is roughly equivalent, I suppose,' Laura said gamely, going along with the joke.

'What does he use for an outback – Richmond Park?' Helen giggled, obviously intent upon sustaining the metaphor.

'No. He doesn't go anywhere – at least I don't think so – so much as not come here.'

Helen pulled a dubious face.

'I think he gets a bit cooped up,' Laura explained apologetically. 'Well, it is a small flat.'

'Cosy.'

'Cosy and small. I know Mike feels it because sometimes he prowls about.'

'Not on all fours?'

'No, not on all fours,' Laura said. Her sister's skittish remarks at Mike's expense were beginning to get on her nerves.

'Sorry, go on.'

'You see, if there are two of you here and one gets

bored with what the other is doing, there isn't really anywhere to go.'

'He could always go for a walk round the window-box,' Helen giggled.

Laura gave her a close look. Helen struggled momentarily to put on a suitably serious face, but failed.

'You're in a really silly mood today, aren't you?' Laura said.

'Yes,' Helen admitted, and smiled broadly. There was an unmistakable twinkle in her eyes and a rather becoming flush to her cheeks that made Laura jump to the inevitable conclusion.

'You're pregnant!' she guessed.

'I think I might be,' Helen said, grinning uncontrollably now.

'Oh, Baby!' Laura said joyfully.

'Oh, baby!' Helen agreed.

They cuddled.

'Why didn't you tell me?'

'I just did.'

'No, straight away. You let me burble on about rotten French novels and Mike prowling and you just sat there. When will you know for sure?'

'I'm going to the doctor's tomorrow.'

'What did Phil say? Is he pleased? Did he give you a cigar?'

'I haven't told him yet.'

'Why ever not?'

'I don't want to tell him until I'm sure.'

'I would.'

'I know you would. You'd have it on *News at Ten*,' Helen laughed.

'Aunt Laura,' Laura said, trying the title for size. 'I can't knit,' she announced sadly.

'I know that.'

'*Aunt* Laura.' It didn't do much for her. 'No, it

makes me sound as if I wear big hairy suits and lisle stockings.'

'No, it doesn't.'

'Auntie Laura.'

'Yes!'

She still wasn't convinced. 'No, that makes me sound like some eccentric old dear who lives in the country.'

'*Uncle* Laura,' Helen suggested, obviously still unable to conquer her silly mood.

'We'll think of something. Oh Helen, I am pleased.'

'Fingers crossed. Anyway I must go,' Helen said, getting up from the couch. 'Now what about this evening?'

'Well, I'd like to come.'

'Then come. We'll pick you up about eight and if your aborigine hasn't turned up by then we'll leave him a note.'

'Yes, all right.'

As Helen reached the door, she turned round. 'Oh, one thing,' she said.

'What?'

'If Mike comes back from his walkabout totally naked except for some body paint, get him to put some clothes on before you bring him out.' She staggered out of the door, laughing hysterically. For some time after the door had closed, Laura could still hear Helen giggling her way downstairs. She smiled affectionately and sat down to resume her work with a sigh.

'*Tante* Laura,' she said out loud, thinking it might sound better in French. It didn't.

Later that evening the unsuspecting father-to-be escorted Helen and Laura to a nearby Italian restaurant for the promised meal. The two conspirators gave each other knowing looks over their drinks. Aunt Laura was literally on the edge of her seat in anticipation of the forthcoming announcement, but, when the second round of drinks arrived and Helen hadn't even steered the conversation into a remotely promising area, she began to get a trifle impatient.

'Why don't you tell him?' she mouthed across the table.

'No,' Helen mouthed back.

'Oh, go on.'

'No.'

'What?' asked Phil

'Nothing,' Helen said quickly, giving her sister a stern look.

Before Phil could press any further, Mike arrived. 'Hello, I got the note,' he said.

'I'm glad you could come,' Helen smiled.

'So what are we celebrating?' Mike asked innocently as he sat down at the table with them.

'Nothing,' Helen said quickly. 'No, we're not celebrating. Just dinner.'

'Oh, well, it's on me anyway,' Mike offered.

'No, we invited you,' Phil insisted.

'I'd like to. I've had some good news.'

Laura looked at him intently. 'What good news Mike?'

'Well, it's the business. I'd almost forgotten what it was like but I'm making a profit again – I'm actually in the black, that's all,' said Mike, who was obviously as pleased as punch.

'Oh Mike, that's smashing,' Laura said, and kissed him in delight.

After shaking hands energetically with his friend, Phil ordered a round of drinks to toast the successful business entrepreneur.

'What a lovely day this is turning out to be,' Laura

said. 'First – ' She broke off in mid sentence as Helen kicked her under the table.

'First what?' Mike asked.

'Oh. First . . .' Laura began,' and now you,' she finished lamely.

Luckily, this elliptical remark seemed to go over Phil's head and he started to quiz Mike about his finances.

'This profit, Mike. Are you going to reinvest?'

'You could do with a new van,' Laura said.

'What about some new clothes?' Helen suggested.

'I could do with some socks,' the entrepreneur announced seriously.

'That's not really thinking big, is it?' Phil said.

'Don't let's get this out of proportion. This is Selway Landscape Gardening we're talking about, not ICI.'

'You've done it on your own, Mike, that's the difference,' Laura said proudly.

'Oh, I don't know. There must have been a Mr I. or Mr C. or another Mr I. originally. Anyway, the thing is that I've already decided what I'd like to do most.'

'What have you decided, Mike?' Laura asked, greatly intrigued.

'Ah. Yes. It's a bit awkward, actually.'

'Why?' asked Phil.

'Well, it's rather rude.'

'You've decided to do something rude?' Helen said incredulously.

'No. The thing is, I'd really like to tell Laura first – on our own.'

Three separate pairs of eyebrows were raised at this, and three separate imaginations started firing on all cylinders. Unused to being the centre of attention, Mike took a casually self-conscious sip of his drink.

'Look, we can always . . .' Phil offered, and stood up as if to leave.

'No, don't be silly,' Laura said. 'We're supposed to be having dinner together. Tell me afterwards, Mike.'

'Yes, that's a better idea,' Mike said with some relief.

'No.' Helen persisted. 'Maybe it's the Camparis, but there's something I'd like to tell Phil as well – privately.'

Now it was Phil's turn to be intrigued. Delighted that the baby was going to be let out of the bag at last, Laura squeezed her sister's hand encouragingly. There was a sudden silence as they all looked at each other foolishly.

'What do we do – whisper?' Mike asked.

Phil stood up. 'This is daft,' he said. 'Look, I'll tell you what. Helen and I will take our drinks over there.' He pointed towards a nearby empty table. 'Then we can whisper at that table, you can whisper at this table and, when we've all whispered what we've got to whisper, we can regroup here, have our dinner and presumably tell each other what we've all been whispering about.'

In the circumstances, this made an odd sort of sense to everyone and, while Helen and Phil took their drinks to the other table, Laura waited expectantly for Mike's rude secret to be revealed to her. He seemed in no particular hurry as he took a slow sip of his drink.

'Here we are, then,' she prompted.

'Yes. Here we are.'

'Hadn't you better start?'

Mike looked over his shoulder as though he feared someone might have crept up on him to eavesdrop on the conversation. 'I don't quite know where to. It needs words, you see, and I never seem able to think of the right ones.'

'Oh, try,' Laura encouraged.

Mike looked over his shoulder again and then started to whisper inaudibly.

'You don't have to whisper. Just talk quietly,' Laura said.

'Right. Well – '

A loud whoop of joy made everyone in the immediate area jump. Mike and Laura turned round to see Phil and Helen embracing each other. At least one of the night's secrets was finally out in the open.

'I hope *you* react like that,' Mike said.

'I don't think you're going to tell me you're pregnant,' Laura laughed.

'Helen?' Mike asked unnecessarily.

'She thinks so.'

'Oh, that's nice. They're just right for kids, those two.'

For a brief moment a wistful look came into Laura's eyes. 'Yes,' she said quietly.

Grinning from ear to ear, the proud father-to-be leaned back in his chair and called over: 'How's your whispering?'

'Oh, sorry. We haven't started yet,' Laura said.

'Oh, no.' Mike realized he'd have to get a move on. 'Well, look, Laura.'

'Yes?'

'We're seeing quite a lot of each other these days,' he continued tentatively.

'Yes.'

'Quite a lot.'

'Yes.'

'Well, now that I've got a bit of money together at last, I think we should put things on a more . . . on a more . . .'

'Permanent basis?' Laura suggested.

'In a way,' he qualified. 'The thing is, I've seen a very nice flat, big enough for two, and I think we should live in it.'

This was it, then. The Marriage Proposal. Not exactly the romantic, heart-stopping marriage proposal a woman would choose to receive from her lover, but then Laura realized that she was dealing with Mike here and not some honey-tongued Lothario. Even though she had no intention of accepting, a strange exhilarating confidence surged through her and in the heat of the moment she was almost tempted to say 'Yes'. She was, if anything, a realistic woman and knew it couldn't possibly work. It was sweet of Mike to ask, and she wanted to reject him without hurting his feelings too much. As she formulated a tender refusal, Phil and Helen bounced over to their table.

'We're going to have a baby,' Phil announced proudly.

'I think Mike's just proposed,' Laura gushed.

There was an unmistakable choking sound from Mike's side of the table.

Back at Laura's flat, Mike poured a fresh cup of coffee and smiled quietly to himself. Laura happened to catch him in mid-smirk. She was definitely *not* smiling.

'I wish you'd stop smirking!' she snapped.

'I can't help it,' Mike said, smirking again. 'Fancy thinking I'd proposed.'

'Yes. Fancy.'

'I expect we shall laugh our heads off about that one day.'

'Let's do it now,' Laura suggested, and laughed mechanically.

'Look, it's not my fault you got hold of the wrong end of the stick.'

'I don't mind being made to look a fool – I look a fool quite often, I suppose. But not an utter fool – not a complete, utter and really silly fool.'

'Well, you shouldn't jump to conclusions. You should have let me finish what I was going to say.'

'You'd taken about three hours to get that far!'

He decided to ignore this outrageous exaggeration. 'About this flat,' he said.

'Ah. Well, the thing is, Mike, I don't really see the point. We're more or less living together already, aren't we?'

'I know, but I thought we might move to larger premises.'

'You make us sound like a ball-bearing factory.'

'It is a bit small, isn't it?'

'It wasn't.'

'It never is at first. The better you know someone, the more room you seem to use.'

'We're not giants,' Laura pointed out.

'We're not pygmies either.'

All this criticism was beginning to make Laura feel rather protective about her little flat. 'It's always been perfectly big enough for me,' she said defiantly.

'That's the point. At least come and see it. See what you think.'

'All right,' she said with some considerable reluctance as she started to clear away the coffee things.

Mike cleared his throat a couple of times. 'Um. Are we living together tonight?' he enquired euphemistically.

'You don't have to ask.'

'I do so long as it's your flat we live in.'

'Mind you, you do pre-empt the answer when you park round the back,' she said tartly.

'Oh.' He shuffled his feet. 'Oh, you noticed that?' he asked sheepishly.

'Oh, I'm quick,' Laura said as she made her way towards the kitchen.

'What would you have said?' he asked out of the blue.

This stopped her in her tracks. 'To what?' she asked innocently.

'You know very well.'

'Now what kind of question is that?'

'Academic.'

'It's a bit late at night to be academic.'

'I'm just curious.'

'All right – no. I'd have said no.'

'Oh,' he said.

If she hadn't known that in Mike's case it was merely a question of pride, Laura would have felt quite sorry for him. 'I've got an academic question for you,' she said.

'What's that?'

'What would you have said if I'd said yes?'

Not expecting an immediate reply, she went into the kitchen to do the washing up, leaving him to mull this over for a while.

Laura allowed herself to be taken to view the flat the following day. She trailed around disconsolately from room to room while Mike enthused over boring details like an embryonic estate agent.

'Nice big windows,' he pointed out.

'I'm not very keen on the view,' Laura said, looking down on the cemetery and crematorium.

'I think it's nice. A bit of green – flowers.'

'But they're in between the gravestones.'

'At least the people across the road won't be noisy,' he joked and, taking her by the arm he guided her into the kitchen. 'Good-sized kitchen, too. Nice work surfaces.'

'I didn't know you were interested in work surfaces.'

'Well, not in a deeply personal sense, no.'

'I don't like the sink,' she carped.

'We'll change it. Well, what do you think?'

Laura wandered aimlessly back into the living-room. Spotting a telephone, she said, 'Is that working? I want to phone Helen.'

'Why? Can't you make your own mind up?'

'I want to see how she got on at the doctor's,' Laura said as she dialled the number.

'Oh, sorry.'

'Hello, Phil? Laura. How does it feel to be a –?' She broke off. 'Oh. Oh Phil, I am sorry. No, of course she doesn't. You look after each other. Yes. Love to Helen. 'Bye, Phil.' Thoughtfully, she replaced the receiver. 'False alarm,' she said. 'And what a horrible expression that is.'

'What a shame,' Mike said. 'Still – ' He was about to resume the tour of the flat when Laura turned towards the front door. 'Where are you going?'

'To see Helen.'

'What about the flat? Are we taking it or not?'

'I can't think about that now.'

'You've got to think about it now. We're first, but there's a queue. If we don't make up our minds, somebody else will have it.'

'Well, of all the callous things to say! You think a flat is more important than a baby.'

'There is no baby,' Mike reminded her gently.

'Well, if you hold human life that cheaply . . .'

'What are you talking about? It's a shame, that's all – a shame. Helen and Phil are young – they'll have thousands of babies if they want them. You know what you're doing? You're just using this as an excuse to wriggle out of making a decision.'

Laura opened her mouth to speak, thought better of it and then slammed out of the flat. Sighing with exasperation, Mike turned away and looked blankly out of the window. The doorbell rang and he went to answer it. Laura marched back into the flat.

'Am I?' she asked.

'Yes,' he answered firmly.

'I don't like the sink,' she demurred.

'You said that.'

'I'd insist on going halves with the rent.'

'You'd have to. I can't afford it on my own.'

'Oh.'

She considered these facts for a while, but still couldn't bring herself to make the all-important decision.

'Well, what do *you* think?' she asked.

'I've told you what I think,' Mike said patiently. 'It's a nice flat. There's plenty of room for two people, and, well, why shouldn't we be the two people?'

'What if we move in and then get on each other's nerves?'

'That wouldn't be the flat's fault. We get on each other's nerves anyway.'

'Not all of the time.'

'Of course not all of the time.'

'I'm getting on your nerves now, aren't I?' she said, watching him closely for the tell-tale signs of irritation.

'Yes, you are, as a matter of fact.'

With an uncanny knack of timing, Mr Bell, the estate agent, walked in. 'How are we doing?' he enquired breezily.

'Getting on each other's nerves,' Laura said.

'Oh. Still, what couple doesn't from time to time? My own good lady, you know, has this habit of cracking her knuckles and sometimes . . .' Mr Bell began to twitch around the mouth. 'But I digress. The thing is, I really must have a decision. Yes or no?'

'Yes,' Laura said.

'No,' Mike said at the same time.

'Sorry?' said Mr Bell.

'Yes,' Laura said, and turned accusingly to Mike.
'You said "No".'

'No', Mike denied.

'I thought you did,' Mr Bell said.

'No, it's the way I speak. When I say "Yes" it often comes out sounding like "No",' Mike gabbled foolishly.

'I see,' Mr Bell said, although he obviously didn't. 'Now are you both sure?'

Mike and Laura looked at each other for a brief moment and then took the plunge.

'Yes,' they said in perfect unison.

Mr Bell seemed satisfied at this joint statement and bustled off to prepare the necessary papers before they changed their minds.

Instinctively, Mike and Laura moved closer together in the centre of the empty room. They both knew that this was a big step.

'Nothing like crossing the old Rubicon to get the adrenalin flowing,' Mike joked uneasily.

'I think we'd better go and sign those papers before we change our minds,' Laura said, feeling suddenly weak at the knees.

'Yes. I'll change that sink,' Mike promised.

'Good.'

'How do you feel?'

'Scared. You?'

'Well, I've had longer to think about it, you see.'

'True.'

'I'm only petrified,' Mike admitted.

Mike and Laura had been living together for almost a week when Mike made an important discovery. It was the new sofa that set him thinking. Only seconds after it was installed in their flat, Mike knew something odd was going on. He stood in the middle of the living room and carefully took stock. Something was missing. In fact, several things were missing.

He looked closely at the new sofa. 'You had a small sofa like this in your old flat,' he said slowly. 'It never arrived here.'

Laura seemed to be suddenly very busy across the other side of the room. 'Well, you know what moving's like. There's always the odd little thing that simply never turns up,' she said dismissively.

This casual acceptance of the loss of an expensive piece of furniture as though it were little more than a mislaid umbrella made Mike slightly suspicious. 'A sofa is not an odd little thing!' He tried to picture the living room in Laura's old flat. 'Wait a minute. There was something else!'

This last remark was apparently lost on Laura, who was concentrating very carefully on the new sofa. 'I think it looks best here,' she said, standing by the window and stretching out her arms in an approximate sofa-like shape.

'I remember not seeing it now,' Mike said.

'You can't remember not seeing something.' She deliberately didn't look at him. 'Do you think it looks best here?'

'A table!' he exclaimed. 'There was a little table!' He headed straight for the bedroom in search of it.

'I do wish you'd help me with this!' Laura shouted after him as she struggled to move the sofa. There was no reply. 'Or maybe here! Mike!' She called after him, more urgently now. Mike returned to the living-room, looking worried.

'The little table's not here either!' he said, prowling around the room. 'And a lamp! There was a little lamp. That's not here.'

'Honestly, Mike, I don't know why you're making such a fuss.'

He looked at her closely. 'I can't understand why

you're not even mildly curious as to why half your furniture has apparently disappeared between your old flat and this flat,' he said.

'Perhaps it was a poltergeist,' she said lightly.

'Oh, very logical!'

Suddenly seeming to tire of this cross-examination, she stalked into the kitchen and reappeared carrying the cutlery drawer.

'All right. Mr Logical! You're so obsessed with making an inventory of everything I own. Here – check the cutlery.' With that she tipped the entire contents of the drawer on the floor in front of him.

Phil and Helen were sitting at the breakfast table, yawning at each other across the toast and coffee.

'Will you stop yawning! You keep setting me off,' Helen said sleepily.

'Sorry. I don't know. I can't take late nights the way I used to.'

'Poor old soul,' Helen said, patting his hand gently.

'What time did we get to bed anyway?'

'About two.'

'And what time did we get to sleep?' Phil asked.

'About four.' Helen smiled at him fondly.

'You're a wicked woman,' Phil admonished.

'True,' said Helen, who was shameless in matters like these.

There was a knock at the back door and Helen got up to answer it. She was somewhat surprised to find Mike standing outside.

'Ah, you're up,' he said.

'Barely.'

'I wanted to catch you before you went to work,' he said to Phil.

'You have, you have,' Phil called out. 'Come in.'

'I won't keep you a minute,' Mike said, stepping

into the kitchen and hovering nervously by the sink. 'I just want to ask you a question.'

'Shoot.'

'Do you happen to remember the name of the removal firm that moved Laura?'

'Do we what?' Helen asked.

'Do you happen to remember – '

'I heard,' Helen interrupted. 'Why ask us?'

'Because I want to know.'

'Why not ask Laura?'

'I did.'

'And?'

'She wouldn't tell me.'

Helen was totally bemused by this, and so was Phil, but he was slowly beginning to recognize all the signs of a Mike-and-Laura shambles and fully intended to remain neutral.

'All right,' Mike said, 'maybe they didn't pinch the stuff but it's gone somewhere.'

Helen frowned. 'What stuff?'

'Oh, bits,' Mike said vaguely. 'Well, I'm not giving up.'

'No, quite,' Phil said, determined to be non-committal.

'Laura wants you to give up something?' Helen probed.

'Well, so she says, but that's not like her at all.' He frowned as he continued his reasoning out loud. 'Now there's something I haven't considered. I suppose it could have just got left behind.'

'Could it?' said Phil, as though he were humouring a lunatic.

'What could?' Helen demanded.

'The stuff. And the new people have just kept it and never said a word. Now that is really charming, isn't it?'

'Terrible,' Phil agreed.

'*What* is?' screamed Helen.

'Them! Of course, they might not have it, in which case I shall look a fool, but it's worth a try, isn't it?'

'Definitely,' Phil said.

'I'll go round there now,' Mike decided.

'Sooner the better, I should think,' 'Phil said.

'Right. Thanks for your help, both of you. I'll let you know how I got on.'

'Good-oh,' Phil said disinterestedly.

'I'll tell you something, though,' Mike said as he reached the door. 'There's something very fishy about all this – very fishy.'

Mike took the stairs to Laura's old flat two at a time. As he approached the landing, he felt a strange sense of urgency mingled with some trepidation. He paused a while to catch his breath and wondered what he should say to the new tenants: should he accuse them outright, or should he bluff his way in on some pretext or other? He walked slowly towards the still familiar door and was puzzled to find it ajar. Tentatively, he pushed it open and walked inside. Laura was standing awkwardly in the middle of the room and seemed not in the least surprised by his sudden and unannounced entrance.

'Hello, Mike,' she said quietly.

'What's going on?' he asked.

'I got here first.'

He looked around the room and immediately recognized the missing articles of furniture that had caused such a scene between them the previous day: the sofa, the table and the lamp stood in a lonely little group in the corner of the room.

'The furniture,' he said. 'That's the furniture that was missing. It did get left.'

'Yes,' Laura said calmly.

'When did you work that out?' he asked.

'I knew all the time.'

'Well, why didn't you just tell me? Why do your nut and chuck cutlery at me for asking where it was?'

'I didn't want you to find out.'

'Oh,' he responded automatically, and then admitted: 'I don't know what it is you didn't want me to find out.'

This was the moment she had been dreading. Laura took a deep breath. 'When we moved into our flat, Mike, I didn't let this one go. I kept it on.'

'Why?'

'Safety, I suppose. In case.'

Very slowly the full implication of this was beginning to sink in. 'And the furniture?' he asked.

'I pop in sometimes,' Laura said.

'A bolt-hole.'

She smiled sadly. 'I wouldn't have put it quite like that.'

Mike suddenly felt he had been badly betrayed. He'd committed himself wholeheartedly to the new flat and their new life together but it seemed that Laura had not. She had been less than open with him. He sat down heavily on the sofa.

Laura noticed that he looked rather pale. 'Would you like some coffee?' she asked, then added apologetically, 'I've got a few things in the kitchen.'

'No, thanks.'

'I suppose I couldn't commit enough, Mike.'

'Obviously,' he said with some bitterness.

'Well, don't look so martyred. You've hardly filled our relationship with any feeling of permanency.'

'I nearly proposed once.'

'When?'

'You were asleep.'

'Oh, wonderful!' she snorted. 'What was I supposed

to do – snore once for "Yes" and twice for "No"? How romantic!'

'I thought we'd come round to romantic. We always come round to romantic.'

'That's because you're not,' she accused.

'And you are?'

'Yes.'

'So you move in with a bloke but keep your old flat on, ready to move out again?'

'Well, when it's said like that . . .'

'How else would you say it?' he demanded.

Laura gave this some thought. She didn't want to write the script for him. She wanted *him* to say the magic words. To make her feel secure and loved. 'I'd say . . .' she started hesitantly, 'I'd say that if the bloke in question took some time – just a little time – to make me feel like a woman . . .'

'What do you mean, "feel like a woman"? You *are* a woman.'

Laura started to interrupt here, but Mike immediately guessed what she was going to say and spoke for her. 'And don't say "Oh, you've noticed." '

'I wasn't going to,' she said quickly, then added: 'I was.'

She slumped down on the sofa beside him. For a long while they stared bleakly ahead.

'We're like a Rubic Cube,' Mike said.

'A what?'

'One of those puzzles – a cube with all different coloured squares. You have to jiggle them about until each side of the cube is all one colour. The best we ever seemed to manage was just one side.'

Laura nodded. 'An eighth.'

'A sixth, actually,' Mike pointed out pedantically.

'Oh, yes.' Something registered with her. ' "Seemed" is a past tense,' she said quietly, knowing

69

what his reply would be but somehow frightened of hearing him put it into words.

'Well, there doesn't seem a lot of point in future tenses, does there?'

'I suppose not.'

'I've just remembered something,' he said, sitting bolt upright.

She looked at him hopefully, silently willing him to say something – anything – that might save the situation. 'What's that?' she asked.

'I'm parked on a double yellow line and I was rude to a traffic warden,' he announced.

If she hadn't felt so close to tears, Laura would have laughed. There was simply no winning with this man.

The dividing up of their possessions was a long and painful process. Laura would have preferred to do the tedious job alone, but Mike insisted on being there to give her a hand. Now it was getting late and several packing cases littered the living-room of their new flat. While Mike went into the kitchen to make some coffee, Laura plodded on with the seemingly endless sorting and wrapping. She sighed as she folded a sheet of newspaper around a china hippopotamus. It seemed such a short time ago – little more than a week – that she had unpacked everything, and now everything had to be uprooted and moved again. Turning her attention to a large pile of books, mostly hers, she was surprised to come across a poetry anthology belonging to Mike.

'I thought you didn't like poetry?' she said, as Mike appeared from the kitchen with two welcome mugs of coffee.

'Oh, that,' Mike said, looking over her shoulder. 'That was my one and only school prize.'

'What for?' Laura asked, intrigued to discover this hitherto unknown side to Mike's character.

'Turning up, I think,' he said dismissively.

'But you must have chosen it. We used to choose our own prizes.'

'No. I wanted *No Orchids For Miss Blandish* but they palmed me off with that,' he shrugged.

They sipped their coffees, and looked around wearily at the general upheaval and disorder.

'Look, I've been thinking about the kitchen sink,' Mike said.

'Why?'

'Well, I gave it to you as a present, so it's yours by right. You should take it with you really.'

'I can't take a sink.'

'I could disconnect it before I go to work in the morning,' Mike offered, obviously very determined that she shouldn't leave the flat without it.

'No, you keep it,' Laura said. 'I can't really say I hope it reminds you of me, but . . .'

This discussion about romantic keepsakes was interrupted by the sudden arrival of Helen and Phil, who turned up carrying a newly opened bottle of champagne and four glasses. Laura took one look at their radiant faces and knew instantly what the celebration was about.

'You are!' she said to her sister.

'I am,' Helen admitted joyfully.

'You're sure this time?'

'Positive.'

'Oh, Baby!'

The two sisters embraced happily, watched by Phil. When they eventually separated, Mike stepped forward to give Helen a kiss, making absolutely sure that he didn't squeeze her too tightly.

Phil handed round the glasses of champagne, and after the flurry of congratulations there was an oddly

71

formal moment. Feeling that such an important occasion should be marked somehow, Laura nudged Mike.

'Oh, yes,' he said reluctantly, and stood to attention. 'Well, I don't know any jokes . . . so to little . . . whatever his or her name will be, who's already a lucky child because his parents love each other very much.' He raised his glass.

This awkward but sincere speech quite touched Phil and Helen, and Laura felt a slow tear begin to trickle down her cheek.

Helen noticed and gave her a quick cuddle. 'You're not supposed to cry,' she said.

'I'm just so happy, that's all,' Laura lied. 'Well, don't stand about – we look like a trade delegation.'

Everyone immediately sat down. It was then that Helen noticed the boxes scattered around the room.

'Laura, what's going on?' she asked in alarm.

'Oh, those.'

'Yes.'

Mike stepped in quickly. 'Decorating,' he said.

Laura nodded in agreement. Phil and Helen found this explanation rather strange.

'I mean, we are going to decorate and I'm a bit of a messy painter especially on the ceilings, so we thought we'd put these things away so they don't get splashed.'

'Why not just cover them up?' Helen asked.

There was no ready answer for this logical suggestion, but Phil stepped in and unwittingly saved their bacon. 'Now that would be the simple thing to do,' he said. 'Have you ever known these two do anything the easy way?'

Mike and Laura did their best to look suitably silly.

'That's us,' Laura said.

Phil stood up. 'Anyway, come on, Mum. We've got another couple of calls to make.'

Helen got to her feet. 'We wanted to tell you first,' she said.

'Blood would have flowed if you hadn't,' Laura said, smiling bravely.

''Bye, Laura. Cheers, Mike. Good luck with the decorating,' Phil said.

'What?' Mike asked, momentarily caught off guard. Laura nudged him. 'Oh yes. What about the champagne?' he asked, noticing the half-empty bottle on the table.

'You two have it,' Helen said. 'I don't think expectant fathers should drink too much. 'Bye.'

Laura gave Helen an extra hug, and the exuberant couple left. After the door had closed behind them, there was an immediate vacuum and a sense of anti-climax.

'That was clever about the decorating,' Laura remarked.

'Well, we couldn't tell them, could we? Not tonight.'

'No,' she agreed.

Alone with each other once more, they both felt a certain unease. Mike remembered the champagne and topped up their glasses. They drank in silence and without enjoyment.

'Did you decide whether you wanted to take the sink or not?' Mike enquired, returning to more mundane matters.

'Oh, do shut up about the sink!' Laura was very close now to breaking down.

'Well, I'd like you to have something.'

'I could hardly put it in a locket, could I?'

Mike finally accepted the fact that Laura didn't want the sink as a memento. Then he had another idea. He picked up his school prize. 'This. Have this,' he said, offering the book to Laura.

'I couldn't take the only school prize you ever won.'

'No, I'd like you to,' he insisted, pressing it on her.

'You see, it's all the things I've never said,' he added quietly.

Laura opened the book at random and read aloud: ' "Half a league, half a league, half a league onward, all in the valley of death rode the six hundred." '

The Selway luck was holding out to the bitter end, Mike thought. Why did she have to pick that particular poem?

'Not in there! Things I've never said.'

'What things?' Laura prompted.

'Well, left out things. I've never said "I love you." '

'Do you?' she asked.

The silence was deafening.

'I don't know,' he finally admitted, refusing to meet her gaze.

'Oh, God!' Laura threw down the book in despair.

'But I don't want you to go,' he asserted.

'Why, Mike? Tell me why?' she asked with pleading eyes.

A beautiful speech trembled on Mike's lips and somehow died on the tip of his tongue. 'Because I don't' was the best he could manage.

Laura shook her head, walked over to one of the tea-chests and knelt down beside it. He watched her helplessly for a while. The moment had passed; it was too late now. Then it dawned on him that she was not adding to the boxes but unwrapping things and taking them out. He walked towards her.

'I never could say no to a smooth talker,' Laura said, looking up at him. They didn't touch each other but both carried on unwrapping the ornaments and setting them down carefully on the table.

4

Helen edged her way slowly downstairs and tottered into the kitchen, where she discovered Phil making a pot of tea and trying to read at the same time.

'You didn't have to get up,' she said, as she summoned up enough energy to give her husband a morning kiss.

'I heard you in the bathroom, so I thought I would.'

She collapsed into a chair and stared wanly at the breakfast table.

'This morning sickness, you know, it's nothing to worry about,' Phil said, putting his arm comfortingly around her hunched shoulders.

'I'm not worried about it. I'm just not terribly keen on it.'

'It says here', Phil announced, referring to the book he was reading, 'that it is probably associated with a high hormone level during pregnancy.'

The fact that there was a scientifically sound reason for her feeling close to death did not exactly concern Helen at this stage of the game. One thing was certain, it didn't make it any easier to bear. 'Does it?' she murmured listlessly.

Unaware of Helen's lack of interest in her biological condition, Phil referred again to his book. 'Yes,' he said authoritatively, 'especially that of progesterone.'

'Really?'

'You mustn't worry, though, because it says here that the vomiting starts to decrease spontaneously about the tenth week of pregnancy, and is usually gone completely by the end of the fourteenth week.'

'Are you making the tea?' she asked, feeling queasy again.

'What? Oh, yes.' Phil reluctantly put his book down for a while.

While Helen sorted desultorily through the morning post, Phil poured out the tea. Noticing that her attention was temporarily distracted, he checked with his book and then measured a spoonful of sugar into her cup.

'There you are,' he said, placing the brew carefully in front of her.

She smiled up at him. 'You are sweet, you know,' she said, beginning to feel more herself again.

'Drink it up.'

'All right.'

He watched with a scientific interest as she took a sip.

'Ughhhhh! There's sugar in this!' she said, pulling a face.

'I know.'

'I don't like sugar in my tea.'

'I know.'

'Then why did you put sugar in it?'

'It says here', Phil observed, turning to the appropriate page of his bible on pregnancy, 'that a small drink of some bland fluid such as sweetened tea, containing a small amount of milk – '

'Give me that,' Helen said, prising the book from her husband's fingers. She scanned the page and then read aloud: 'It says that one of the best methods of controlling the sickness is to have a small drink of some bland fluid . . . and so on and so on.'

'Yes, I know.'

'But I've already been sick! What's the point of

trying to make me drink this to control it when I've already done it?'

Phil thought about this for a moment. 'Oh, yes, I see,' he admitted reluctantly. 'I'll wake you up with a cup tomorrow,' he promised.

'You will not! Sugar in my tea makes me feel sick.'

'It's a vicious circle, isn't it?'

He said this in such a serious tone of voice that it made Helen laugh. 'It's a terrible responsibility, isn't it, being the only couple in the world ever to have a baby?' she said. Then, feeling better already, she got up and threw the sweetened tea down the sink. Taking some clean cups from the cupboard, she poured them both some fresh tea.

Surreptitiously, Phil reached for his book to check up on some further facts, but Helen saw the move and quickly changed the subject. 'What's in the post?' she asked.

'Oh, nothing special,' he said, sorting through the mail. 'Oh yes, there is. There's a card from your mum and dad.' He handed it to her.

While she was looking at it, he considered sneaking a small amount of sugar into her cup, but thought better of it.

'Oh, they're coming up tomorrow,' Helen said.

'Fine.'

'No, just a minute,' she corrected herself, looking at the date stamp. 'This was posted yesterday, so tomorrow doesn't mean tomorrow, it means today. They're coming up today.'

'Well, that's all right,' Phil shrugged. 'It's Saturday.'

'Yes,' Helen said doubtfully.

'What's the matter?'

'It's the PS "Looking forward to meeting Mike".'

'Well, they would be,' Phil reasoned, missing a crucial point.

77

'Yes,' she said, looking worried.

'They must know about him by now.'

'Yes. But knowing about Mike and meeting him aren't the same thing.' She got up quickly. 'I'd better phone Laura.'

'What are you going to do? Get her to hide him under the floorboards till they've gone?'

'I'd better phone Laura,' Helen repeated, beginning to panic on her sister's behalf.

'It's only meeting someone. I mean, they'd never met me until they met me, had they?'

'They couldn't have really, could they?'

'You know what I mean.'

'Yes, but you had them eating out of your hand in five minutes flat.'

'True,' Phil agreed, unashamedly immodest. 'Still, they're not ogres, are they? If their eldest daughter has finally got herself a . . . a . . . um . . .' – he paused, unable to define Mike's exact status in life – 'bloke, they're naturally going to want to meet him.'

'Yes.'

'See what he's like.'

'Yes.'

'It's very early.'

'I know.'

'It's just a meeting.'

'I know.'

Phil recognized the potential for disaster. He walked over to the phone, took the receiver off the hook and held it out to Helen.

'I think you'd better phone Laura,' he said.

Laura felt the unmistakable symptoms of the beginnings of a bad headache. Only several minutes had elapsed since the phone call from Helen announcing her parents' forthcoming visit, and she was starting

78

to brood. Her mother and father always had this debilitating effect upon her. She felt awkward in their company because Helen was their firm favourite and, no matter how hard she tried, Laura always managed to be a constant disappointment to them. She bore no ill-will towards her sister because of this favouritism – she'd lived with it for too long and it had now become a fact of life – but sometimes, just sometimes, she wished she could do something that would please her parents and make them proud of her. Now, of course, there was the added complication of Mike – he was not the sort of bloke who was going to make an immediately favourable impression on anyone, least of all . . . She shook her head. In order to concentrate her mind on other things, she got out the vacuum cleaner and started to do some housework, but it was a haphazard enterprise and she soon found her mind wandering to the forthcoming 'ordeal'. It was only when the vacuum cleaner began making strange gurgling noises that she realized she was holding the nozzle at waist height and was in the process of sucking up the tablecloth. She was busy retrieving it when Mike walked in.

'I've got the papers,' he said.

'You were a long time.'

'Yes, I know.'

'Did you walk?'

'No, I took the van. It would have been quicker to walk. It got stuck in first gear.' He sat down. 'I was being overtaken by children on skates.'

Laura made a deep, inner effort and then, assuming a false brightness, said: 'Never mind. I've had a nice surprise.'

'Oh?'

'Yes. Helen phoned. My mum and dad are coming up today.'

'Oh,' Mike said, trying to sound as though this were the good news he had been waiting for all week.

'We can go over to Helen and Phil's for lunch and you can meet them.'

'That would be very nice,' Mike said politely.

'Yes. Smashing, isn't it?' she said, smiling broadly.

'Smashing,' he echoed.

'I'm ever so pleased.'

'Yes. Me too. I've been wanting to meet them.'

'Oh, I've been wanting you to meet them,' she lied. 'I've been meaning to ask them up, but you know how time slips by.'

'Oh, it does, yes. It does slip by. Still, this solves the problem, doesn't it?'

'Absolutely. It's perfect really.'

'Yes. I've been wanting to meet them.'

By this time they were beginning to sound like characters out of a Pinter play. Laura looked at Mike and Mike looked at Laura; they both knew they could no longer keep up the pretence. She sat down beside him.

'I could phone Helen and say we've got to go somewhere,' she offered.

'It would only be putting if off,' Mike said, bravely grasping the nettle.

She looked at him fondly. 'You're right. I'm sorry, Mike.'

'You don't have to apologize for having parents.'

'No. They're very nice really.'

'Why are you looking so gloomy then?'

'I'm thinking of you.'

'Thanks.'

'You know what I mean. Meeting peeople isn't your favourite sport at the best of times – let alone parents.'

'You don't think they'll like me,' he guessed.

'I didn't say that.'

'Approve of me?'

'No. Anyway, it's not for them to approve or disapprove of you. I mean, here we are together.' She was beginning to feel a little on the aggressive side now. 'You're a fact of my life. Now if they don't like it, well, that's just too bad.'

'You don't think they will, do you?'

She sighed. 'I don't know, Mike. It's me. I'm not sure I've ever quite fitted their picture of a daughter – especially with Helen as a sort of definitive edition. Oh, blow it! It's not as though you're some pimply youth asking for my hand, is it?'

'Right. Actually, I was very lucky with pimples,' Mike said gravely.

'Were you?'

'Yes. I only ever had one.' He made a circle with his thumb and fingers. 'About that big,' he grinned, and was gratified to see that he had made Laura smile and relax. 'I'll do my best,' he promised. 'I won't turn up wearing a torn singlet and carrying a crate of brown ale or anything like that.'

Laura began to worry again. 'No. I don't want you to *do* anything, Mike. Just be yourself – and feel relaxed about the whole thing.'

Mike looked at Laura's worried face. 'Like you are,' he said.

'This is silly.'

'I know. Well . . . I'd better have a look at the van.'

'Can you fix it?'

'I hope so. First impressions, you know.'

They both had an identical subliminal picture of Mike's dirty and battered old van drawing up outside Helen and Phil's house.

'Even if I did fix it,' Mike said doubtfully.

'Yes,' Laura said. 'Let's go by bus.'

'Better.'

*

Later that morning, a relaxed and cosy domestic scenario was being played out in Phil and Helen's living-room. Mr and Mrs Dalton were happily ensconced and beaming fondly at their daughter and son-in-law. It was obvious at a glance that, while Helen took after her vivacious, slim mother, Laura had inherited her father's more sombre, heavy looks.

Helen was holding a plastic rugby ball and trying hard not to laugh. 'It's very nice, Dad,' she said, 'but don't you think it's a bit previous?'

'I told him,' Mrs Dalton said knowingly. 'He wouldn't listen.'

'There's no harm in getting the boy off on the right foot,' Mr Dalton said seriously.

Helen looked across to Phil for an opinion. She should have known better. He was totally in agreement with her father and was exchanging looks with him – the looks of men who had stood shoulder to shoulder at Twickenham.

'You don't know it will be a boy,' she said.

'Phil seems very confident,' Mr Dalton pointed out dogmatically.

'Oh, does he?'

'Yes. We're going to call him Bill,' Phil announced.

A wild, almost fanatical gleam came into Mr Dalton's eyes. 'After Bill Beaumont?' he asked.

'Naturally,' Phil confirmed.

'That does it. I'm going to have a girl,' Helen said.

'Quite right,' her mother agreed. 'And she won't grow up to be England's first woman prop forward, whatever they think.'

'Boy,' Phil insisted.

'William Beaumont Barker,' Mr Dalton said reverentially.

'I like that,' Phil said.

Mother and daughter looked at one another in amused resignation. 'What time are Laura and her young man coming?' Mrs Dalton enquired, changing the subject.

This definition of Mike amused Helen. 'Young man?' she laughed.

'Well . . . what do you call him?'

'Mike,' Helen said.

'Don't be silly, Helen.'

'Well, I don't know. None of us has ever been quite sure what to call him.'

'I thought we'd settled on "friend",' Phil said.

' "Friend"!' Mrs Dalton said, wrinkling up her nose in distaste.

The conversation was getting rather out of hand, and Helen decided to take her mother off to the kitchen out of harm's way. Mr Dalton waited until the door had safely closed behind them and then turned to Phil.

'She worries,' he confided.

'They do.'

'Is Laura happy?'

'You're worried as well,' Phil noticed with some amusement.

'She's got the brains, Laura, but with people nothing's ever been easy.'

'I get the same feeling about Mike.'

Mr Dalton looked at him closely.

'Mind you, he's a good bloke,' Phil said. 'Bit weird sometimes.'

'Weird?' said Mr Dalton, latching on to the word.

'No, not weird. Odd,' Phil qualified.

'Odd?'

'No, not really odd. What's the word I'm looking for?'

'I shudder to think. How much do you really know about him?'

'Well, let's see.' Phil thought for a moment and then admitted: 'Very little really.'

'May I have a drink?' Mr Dalton asked, beginning to feel distinctly edgy now.

'Yes, of course,' Phil said, getting to his feet. At that moment there was a ring at the doorbell. 'That must be them,' he said as he went to answer the door. He was rather surprised when Laura, unaccompanied by Mike, walked in.

'Hello, Laura,' he said.

'Hello, Phil, hello, Daddy,' Laura said breathlessly.

'Hello, Dumpling,' Mr Dalton said.

Laura winced perceptibly at this pet name but kissed her father dutifully.

'Where's Mike?' Phil asked, looking out of the front door and down the path.

'Ah! He got left on the bus,' Laura replied airily, as though this were a perfectly natural occurrence. She deliberately didn't look at her father as she said this, but she immediately sensed his disapproval. 'I know it sounds silly, but, you see, we got off and a lady was getting on with a pram, so Mike helped her on with the pram but the bus pulled away before he could get off again.'

'I see,' Mr Dalton said slowly. He was beginning to realize that Phil's assessment of Mike was a fairly accurate one.

Mrs Dalton came bustling out of the kitchen and gave Laura a loud kiss. 'Where's your young . . . your friend?' she asked, looking around as though she expected him to be hiding behind the curtains.

'He got left on the bus,' Laura said.

'Did you have him wrapped in something?'

'No, he was helping a lady with a push-chair.'

'Pram,' Phil corrected.

'Yes. Pram – push-chair – sort of thing. Anyway, Mike didn't have time to get off again.'

'Couldn't he have rung the bell?' Mr Dalton said.

'Oh, I don't know if he thought of that,' Laura said.

There was a stupified silence at this remark.

'He'll get off at the next stop,' Laura said.

'Who will?' Helen asked as she entered the room.

'Mike,' Laura said wearily, waiting for the inevitable question.

'Why didn't he get off at the same stop as you?'

'It's a long story,' Laura said, gritting her teeth.

'Let's all have a drink,' Phil suggested. 'He'll be here in a minute.'

While Phil poured everyone a large sherry, Mrs Dalton turned to Laura and asked, 'What do you think of your little sister, then?'

'She's all right,' Laura said, her mind on other things.

'The baby!'

'Oh, the baby. I'm very pleased, naturally.'

'I'm glad one of our daughters is going to give us a grandchild,' her mother said pointedly.

'I've hardly got through the door!' Laura snapped, beginning to feel the return of her headache.

'Yes, come on,' Helen urged. 'Don't let's start talking about the baby again. We've got months to talk about the baby. Let's talk about Laura and Mike.'

'If we talk about Mike, we'll be talking about him behind his back, because he got left on the bus,' Mr Dalton pointed out. By this time, Laura was beginning to feel responsible for the whole incident.

Phil opened the front door and looked out. 'There's still no sign of him.'

'Doesn't he have a car?' Mrs Dalton asked.

'He's got a van,' Laura said.

If Laura had said he had a donkey cart, her mother's reaction could hardly have been more disparaging. 'A van?' she repeated, wrinkling up her face in distaste.

'Yes, but it's stuck in first gear at the moment.'

'I see.' Mr and Mrs Dalton exchanged glances.

Helen gave Laura's hand a comforting squeeze.

Half an hour and another round of sherries later, Mike was conspicuous by his absence. Phil made repeated journeys to the front door and eventually decided to leave it ajar. Laura was beginning to feel increasingly tense.

'He would have got off at the next stop, wouldn't he?' Phil asked.

'Of course he would,' Laura said, although by this time she was beginning to have grave doubts.

'Well, where is he?' Mrs Dalton asked.

'I don't know,' Laura said, trying to keep the irritation out of her voice.

'He wouldn't have repeated the pram thing, would he?' Mr Dalton said this as though he was under the impression that Mike had a fetish about baby conveyances.

'He does not go around looking for people with prams to help on to buses,' Laura said.

'Well, where is he?' Mrs Dalton repeated annoyingly.

'I do wish you'd think of another question,' Laura snapped.

'Your manners don't improve with age, Laura,' her mother chided.

'And neither does your imagination, if all you can think of saying is "Well, where is he?" ' Her mother and father gave her a warning look at this. 'I'm sorry,' Laura apologized, feeling about eight years old.

'I just don't want Helen's lunch to spoil,' her mother said.

'Mum, it's salad. It can't spoil,' Helen pointed out.

Mrs Dalton smiled fondly at her favourite daughter. 'You always go to so much trouble,' she said lovingly.

'Look here,' Mr Dalton said. 'How far away is the next bus stop?'

'Oh ... about half a mile, I suppose,' Phil estimated.

Mr Dalton looked at his watch and everyone in the room started a private time-and-distance problem.

Suddenly, Phil heard a noise outside. 'That's the gate. It must be Mike,' he said, getting up and going towards the half-open front door. 'Come in, Mike. We'd given you up,' Laura, with some relief, heard him say.

The wanderer made his entrance, his head tilted back at a forty-five-degree angle, and a blood-stained handkerchief clasped to his nose. 'Hello, Sorry. Nose-bleed. Bathroom,' he mumbled, and hurried straight through the living-room and up the stairs.

Everyone stared after him. Laura put her aching head in her hands and prayed for the ground to swallow her up. No one, not even her mother, could think of anything to say, and there was a stunned silence. Laura knew that sooner or later one of her parents was going to ask an unanswerable question and, in order to avoid further interrogation about Mike's travelling adventures, she quickly excused herself and followed him upstairs into the bathroom where she helped him take off his blood-stained shirt and apply a wet cloth to his bleeding nose. After a few minutes, Mike was able to assume an upright position.

'Stopped?' she asked.

'I think so.'

Phil came in, carrying a clean shirt for Mike to put on. 'Stopped?' he asked.

'I think so,' Mike said.

'There's a clean shirt.'

'Ta. I got blood on my tie, too.'

'I'll just pop back to Menswear,' Phil joked, and went out again.

Mike put on the clean shirt and buttoned it up. 'What a shambles,' he muttered. 'What an entrance.'

'Whatever happened?' Laura asked.

'Well, I helped the lady on with the pram . . .'

'I mean after that.'

'Oh. Well, I went to get off at the next stop but the conductor wanted excess fair by then, you see. But I didn't have any change. I only had a five-pound note. So the conductor got stroppy and there was a sort of scuffle.'

'You didn't fight the conductor?' Laura asked incredulously.

'No. Some other chap in a trilby said that I shouldn't have to pay the excess fare anyway because the conductor should have stopped the bus when I wanted to get back off after I helped on the lady with the pram.'

'But why is your nose bleeding?'

'Because the conductor lunged at the chap in the trilby who was sticking up for me, and the chap in the trilby put his arms up to defend himself and hit me on the nose with his elbow.'

'Oh dear,' was all Laura could find to say.

'Oh dear, indeed. I've got things off to a really good start, haven't I?'

'It's not your fault.'

'Well, what is it then?'

'The way of things,' she said in resignation.

Phil popped back with one of his ties. 'What happened to your nose, Mike?' he asked.

Not wanting to retail the entire sordid episode again, Mike concentrated on the highlights. 'Some chap who was taking my part in a row hit me with his elbow.'

Phil was confused but not exactly surprised. With Mike anything was feasible. 'Yes, but . . . no, I won't ask,' he said. 'Here, put this on' – and he handed Mike his tie.

'Thanks, Phil.'

'Look, I'm on your side, you know – both of you. It's always a bit hairy the first time. Just try to relax.'

'That's what I said this morning,' Laura agreed.

'Well, there you are, then,' Phil said.

'Saying is one thing,' Laura sighed. 'Right now I'd feel more relaxed if I were to nose-dive off the Forth Bridge.'

'I'll tell them you're coming,' Phil said.

'I shouldn't,' Mike said ruefully. 'The way things are going, I'll probably fall down the stairs.'

Meanwhile, in the kitchen, Helen was trying to smooth the way by giving her mother some daughterly advice. Mrs Dalton didn't seem to be taking it very well.

'Favouritism? I have never shown favouritism to either of my children in my life,' she bristled.

'You have, Mum,' Helen said, 'and it's to me. And you're still doing it. All this wonder at giving you grandchildren.'

'Well, you are.'

'I know, but it's not a present. Now come on – be good. This is difficult enough for Laura as it is.'

'It's not of our making entirely,' Mr Dalton said. 'If Laura *will* move in with some fellow who can't even get off a bus.'

'Dad, one more mention of that, and your grand-child – of whatever sex – will never be allowed near a rugby ball in his or her life – now that's a promise.'

This terrible threat gave Mr Dalton serious pause for thought, and he shut up immediately.

Phil came in and announced the imminent arrival of Mike and Laura. An expectant hush fell on the room. Shoulder to shoulder, Mike and Laura made their entrance. Uneasily, they stood for a while wedged in the door.

'Here we are,' Laura said.

'Here they are!' Helen announced. She gestured like a conjuror's assistant drawing the audience's attention to the completion of a spectacular trick.

Laura stepped forward. 'So. Mum – Dad. I'd like you to meet Mike,' Laura announced formally.

'Mike,' Mrs Dalton said, smiling warily.

'Mrs Dalton,' Mike replied.

'Mike,' Mr Dalton said.

'Mr Dalton,' Mike replied.

Introductions over, they sat down to lunch.

'Right. Fall to,' Phil said in evident relief.

There was a brief silence as everyone dutifully tucked into the salad.

'This is delicious, Helen,' Mrs Dalton said, almost before she had taken the first mouthful of lettuce.

'Good,' Helen said, and gave her mother a warning look.

'Of course,' Mrs Dalton added, 'Laura's cooking was always nice too.'

'It was horrible,' Laura said.

'Not all of it.'

'You used to make me little jam tarts,' Mr Dalton reminisced. 'Dirty little finger-marks all over the pastry.'

'Did you eat them?' Laura asked impassively.

'Some of them,' he said, swallowing hard at the memory.

'Laura's chips are very good, you know,' Mike observed. 'Very good indeed.'

Mrs Dalton looked at him in utter disbelief. 'Well, there you are, then,' she said.

Feeling that the time was right to get on a 'man-to-man' footing with his daughter's 'young man', Mr Dalton turned to Mike and pointed to his tie. 'That's a rugby club tie, isn't it?'

'Is it?' Mike said, looking down at the borrowed tie in evident surprise.

'Isn't it?' Mr Dalton said, totally confused by now.

'I don't know,' Mike confessed.

'What?' Mr Dalton said.

'I lent it to him,' Phil explained. 'Mike's was a bit gory.'

'From the nose,' Mike said.

'Do you often get nose-bleeds?' Mrs Dalton asked suspiciously.

'Only if I get elbowed in the face,' Mike replied, deciding to keep things as simple as possible.

'I see,' she said, staring at him as though he were some kind of dangerous, unexploded firework that might decide to go off at any moment.

'Have you ever played rugby, Mike?' Mr Dalton asked.

'No.'

'Oh.' This came as a bitter blow to Mr Dalton.

'That's a coincidence,' Helen said brightly, desperately trying to break new ground.

'What is, love?' Phil asked.

'The coincidence? I was just thinking that Mike and Laura first met in this very house.'

'So they did. You did, didn't you?' Phil said.

'Yes, we did,' Laura admitted.

'We did,' Mike said. 'We couldn't stand each other at first. Then we got chatting in the bedroom and . . .' He broke off, aware that he had inadvertently given the wrong impression.

'We're very broadminded,' Mrs Dalton said, in the tone of voice that indicated otherwise.

'It wasn't that kind of a chat,' Laura said, aware that her denial only served to make matters worse.

'And how long have you been living together?' her father enquired.

'About a month – and I think that if either of you has anything to say about it you'd better say it now,' Laura declared, immediately on the defensive.

'Oh, no. So long as you're happy,' Mr Dalton said.

'People *do* nowadays,' Mrs Dalton remarked. 'Some of them,' she added.

'Right,' Phil said. 'Helen and I would if we weren't married.'

'Would we?' Helen said.

Phil instantly realized he was in hot water. 'No, I mean we might have if we hadn't decided to get married,' he qualified.

Mrs Dalton smiled at them benignly. 'But you *did* decide.'

'Well, bully for them! Can't we change the subject?' Laura said tartly.

'Yes, let's,' Helen agreed.

'What about your parents, Mike? Where do they live?' Mr Dalton enquired.

'I haven't the faintest idea,' Mike replied.

This came as a big surprise to everyone except Laura. 'Mike was left, you see,' she said.

'Oh, Mike,' Helen said, tears springing to her eyes.

'Not in a handbag at Victoria Station or anything. Just left,' he explained.

'I'm so sorry,' Mrs Dalton said.

'Have you no idea who they were?' Mr Dalton asked.

'No. A man and a woman presumably,' Mike said.

'Oh, Mike,' Helen repeated, restraining herself from taking him in her arms and cuddling him.

Mike was aware that everyone had stopped eating and was looking at him intently. 'It's all right,' he said.

'It's not. It's sad,' Helen said.

'I'm so sorry,' Mrs Dalton said.

'Poor old fellow.' Mr Dalton patted him on the back in a fatherly fashion.

'Whose idea was it to change the subject?' Mike asked, beginning to feel rather foolish.

'Mine,' Laura said.

'Certainly cheered things up, didn't it?'

'Alice and Tom,' Laura said for at least the tenth time since they had arrived back at their flat.

'Well, that's their names,' Mike said.

'I know. I just couldn't ever have imagined you calling them Alice and Tom,' she said, shaking her head in disbelief.

'I could never have imagined that either.'

'They certainly warmed up after lunch, didn't they?' Mike said.

'Of course, I'd like to think that my personal charm finally won them over, but I suppose that, if I'm honest, the orphanage turned out to be my trump card.'

'We must remember that in future,' Laura observed thoughtfully.

'Perhaps I should have tried it on the bus conductor,' Mike said. 'Well, what shall we do this evening?'

'What were we going to do this afternoon?'

'Nothing,' he said contentedly.

'Let's do that.'

'Good idea.' Mike put his arm around her and they cuddled up to each other on the couch.

'They are nice, you know, your mum and dad,' Mike said.

'I know. It's just that they . . .'

'They worry about you.'

'With good reason, I suppose. I know I've been a disappointment, but they make not giving them grandchildren sound like pure meanness of spirit.'

'And, let's face it, anyone who has Helen for a sister . . . well it's tremendous competition, isn't it?'

'Yes. If she wasn't so nice, I'd really hate her.'

'You're better.'

'Nicer?'

'No, better. If you get something right, it's not because of any intrinsic rightness in you, it's because you've tried.'

Laura gave this some serious thought. 'Is that profound?' she asked.

'I'm not sure.'

'I'll tell you something.'

'Profound?'

'Not very. I feel ashamed of ever being jealous of Helen. All right, she's favourite – well, somebody has to be. But we both had lots of love. You couldn't have.'

'Oh, I did. It was just from a lot of different people, that's all. Auntie This . . . Mrs That. Not the same people all of the time though.' He remembered something. 'Kingsley Amis was a Barnardo's Boy, you know.'

'Was he?' Laura said doubtfully.

'Yes.'

'Are you sure?'

'Yes.'

Mike made a quick mental calculation. Was it Kingsley Amis who wrote *The Virgin Soldiers*? No. 'Leslie Thomas, that's who I mean,' he corrected himself.

'You've never really talked about it, you know.'

'If I'm honest, I don't remember that much. I remember more about being a grown-up than a child.'

'You must remember something.'

He looked at her earnest face looking up at him. He couldn't resist it. Clearing his throat he said, 'There was a Christmas . . .' Laura took his hand and squeezed it comfortingly. 'I must have been about six,' he said, striving to remember. 'We were all taken to a big store to see Father Christmas. He smelled of peppermints, I remember that. I was quite frightened in his grotto because it was quite dim in there. Anyway, he sat me on his lap and he asked me what I'd like best in the world for Christmas. And do you know what I asked for?'

Laura swallowed hard as she felt a lump rising in her throat. 'A mother and father?' she said.

Mike paused for effect, then said: 'No. A little pair of shoes for my little bare feet and a coat for my little bare back.'

Laura picked up a cushion and hit him repeatedly around the head.

5

Selway Landscape Gardening. The very name conjured up vistas of softly rolling lawns, intricately planned rockeries and colourful flower-beds. In reality, things were – to coin a gardening phrase – rather more down to earth. The Selway Landscape Gardening centre consisted of a ramshackle wooden shed, standing forlornly in a cluttered yard. It was a shoestring enterprise and, although Mike was a good gardener, he had neither the time nor the money for window-dressing. He worked long, hard hours aided by the redoubtable Charlie, an irascible old Cockney who was constantly threatening to unionize the business. As Charlie was the only worker Mike could afford to employ, these threats of unionization were never carried out and Charlie had to content himself with dark mutterings about tea-breaks, job demarcation and rates of pay.

Luckily, the majority of Mike's clients did their business by phone; if they had called round in person they might conceivably have had second thoughts. There was a time when the 'office' or shed was virtually indistinguishable from the yard outside: giant bags of peat and compost sagged over the floor, gardening tools littered the desk top, and the filing cabinet was full of assorted flower-pots and seed propagators. Since Laura had come into his life, Mike's premises had taken on a more ordered existence. She and Helen had spent a whole day happily reorganizing things – much to Charlie's disgust – and now the place was almost presentable, in a homely sort of way.

It was one of those Mondays when nothing seemed to be working – Charlie certainly wasn't, and Mike was trying to cope on his own. For the last ten minutes he had been struggling to lift a heavy motor mower from the back of his van. His makeshift ramps of two boards had snapped under the weight and he had improvised, rather cleverly he thought, with two large bales of peat. After a massive effort, he'd managed to bump the mower down from the van on to the bales and was psyching himself up to heave it down the rest of the way when Laura arrived at the yard.

'What are you doing?' she asked, looking at the mower wedged awkwardly on top of the peat bags.

'Oh, it's a sort of initiative test,' Mike explained wearily.

'Come inside and have some tea,' she said.

'That's a better idea altogether,' Mike said with evident relief and, giving the mower one last warning look, he followed her into the office.

As Laura busied herself with the tea things, Mike slumped down on the chair behind the desk.

'Tired?' Laura asked.

'A little bit.'

'Hungry?'

'Yes, I am actually.'

Laura delved deep into her shopping bag and brought out a large tin. 'I've made a cake,' she said, easing it out of the tin and setting it down gingerly on the desk in front of Mike. He eyed it warily. 'Not *that* hungry?' she said, looking at his face.

As with the rest of Laura's cooking, her cake-making left a great deal to be desired. One thing was sure – Laura's cakes were never dull. No two were quite the same, and they constantly surprised with their flavour and texture.

'No,' Mike protested, 'they're getting better all the time, your cakes, all the time. Really.'

Laura cut two generous slices and handed one to Mike. Anxiously she looked on as he took an experimental bite. He nodded appreciatively at first, but the chewing seemed to take rather longer than it should.

'Does it go on a bit?' she asked after a full minute had passed.

'A bit,' Mike mumbled, chewing doggedly. He eventually managed to wash it down with some tea and Laura braved a bite out of her slice. Her 'appreciation' was slightly more honest than Mike's.

'I could be sent to prison for experimenting on you like this,' she declared grimly. She pushed the remains of the cake away and then said anxiously, 'Mike, there's a weekend course I'd like to go on.'

'You don't need to go on a course,' he protested. 'I'm not really that fond of cake, anyway.'

'Not a cookery course. Well, it's a seminar really on "Efficiency Principles in Stock Control" – and it's international and they need interpreters and I've been offered a job,' she said in one breath.

'Where is it?'

'Worthing. It would mean a weekend away, but the money's good. What do you think?'

'You don't have to ask my permission.'

'I'm not asking your permission. I'm asking you what you think.'

'Well, if the money's good,' he said.

'You don't want me to go, do you?'

This was slightly dodgy territory and Mike was being very careful not to venture a firm opinion either way. 'It's up to you,' he said vaguely.

'I don't have to go.'

'All right, don't go.'

'I knew you didn't want me to,' she said with just a trace of satisfaction.

Mike looked heavenwards. There was no winning sometimes where women were concerned. 'I said it's up to you,' he repeated.

'All right. I'll go, then,' she said, but without any real conviction.

'Fine.'

'More tea?' she asked, picking up the teapot.

'Yes please.'

'Mostly blokes, I suppose, at this seminar?' Mike asked casually.

'Mostly. I can't see "Efficiency Principles in Stock Control" really fascinating a lot of women.'

An idea occurred to him. 'Well, why don't I come with you? I could do with a couple of days at the seaside.'

'But I'd be working during the day,' she warned.

'I could bring my bucket and spade.'

'It's pebbles at Worthing.'

'All right. Just my bucket. I could collect pebbles.'

Laura considered the prospect for a while. The idea had its good points. Hotels could be lonely places for a single woman. On the other hand, there were definitely pitfalls – particularly with Mike around. 'I wouldn't want you to be bored,' she said.

It was his turn to be difficult now. 'You don't want me to come, do you?' he said.

'I do, I do. I think it's a lovely idea. I've been on this type of thing before and I've never had company.'

'You did when you went to Brussels,' Mike said darkly. 'You met that Ben.'

She didn't really need to be reminded of this unhappy episode in her life. 'Oh. Yes. That was before we . . .'

Mike felt a bit mean dragging this up. 'Yes, I know.'

'That was a shambles.'

'Won't be this time,' he said cheerfully. 'You'll have Mr Smooth along.'

There was a loud crash from the yard and they both jumped.

'What was that?' Laura asked.

Mike got up and looked out of the window. 'Mr Smooth's mower has just fallen off two bales of peat,' he said.

The hotel where the conference was being staged was an impressive Victorian building facing the sea front, and when Mike and Laura trundled up to the entrance in the van they were greeted by an impressively disdainful uniformed flunkey.

Mike climbed out of the van on the passenger side. 'Afternoon' he said casually.

'Good afternoon, sir – madam,' the doorman said grudgingly. 'Do you have any luggage?' The tone of voice clearly implied that the doorman was expecting, at the very best, a pathetic carrier bag containing a toothbrush and assorted nightwear.

'In the back,' Mike said.

Opening up the back of the van with a flourish, the doorman was confronted by a bewildering array of gardening impedimenta and by peering into the gloom he was just able to discern two suitcases wedged in between a couple of bags of John Innes potting compost. Assuming a suitably disgusted look, he gave a lofty signal to the porter, who hauled out the cases and carried them into the hotel. Mike and Laura started to follow but were called back.

'Excuse me, sir,' the doorman said, indicating the van with a gloved finger. 'This.'

'Yes?'

'The car park is at the rear of the hotel.'

'Good. Stick it round there for me, would you?' Mike said, tossing him the keys with a grin.

Laura looked at Mike approvingly and then turned to the doorman to offer some advice. 'And you have to get in the passenger side and climb across, so mind your hat,' she said airily.

Feeling rather pleased with the way they'd handled things, Mike and Laura swept up the steps into reception. Mike was about to register at the desk when Laura tugged him back by the sleeve of his jacket.

'Mike,' she whispered, looking around nervously, 'when I made the reservation I thought ... Well, we're Mr and Mrs Selway.'

'Why?'

'Well,' she said, and gave him a meaning look.

He immediately caught her drift. 'Yes. Probably better.'

Together, they walked up to the desk where the porter was waiting with their suitcases.

The middle-aged male receptionist greeted them efficiently. 'Good afternoon, sir. Good afternoon, madam.'

'Afternoon,' Mike said breezily. 'We have a reservation – Mr and Mrs Selway.'

'Yes, sir. If you'd care to register,' the receptionist said smoothly, handing him a pen.

Mike signed them both in. To his surprise, he was feeling rather giggly by this time and Laura, who had also caught the mood, was fighting hard not to laugh out loud. They were extremely careful not to catch each other's eye.

'Room 504,' the receptionist said to the porter. Then he turned to Mike and Laura. 'May I ask if either or both of you are here for the seminar?'

'Yes, I am actually,' Laura said.

'Ah. Then we have a lapel badge and an itinerary for you,' he told her, sorting through a box file containing several official envelopes. After a few seconds, a thought occurred to Laura. The same thought also occurred to Mike: 'Mrs Selway' was not going to be among the names. They looked at each other guiltily. Unaware of this complication, the receptionist was still busy searching for the non-existent envelope. 'Selway . . . Selway . . .' he muttered. 'That's strange . . .' He started to go through the file once more.

Laura cleared her throat. 'I . . . I might be there as Laura Dalton, actually.'

He looked up. 'Laura Dalton?' he queried.

'Yes.'

He looked at Mike and then looked at Laura. 'I see,' he said, and smiled.

'It's a name I use sometimes . . . a professional name,' Laura said, feeling herself blushing stupidly.

'Yes, of course,' the receptionist said smoothly, and smiled again. 'Ah, there we are,' he said, finding the enveloped and handing it to Laura. 'Mrs Selway. Laura Dalton.'

Laura Dalton, alias Mrs Selway, smiled weakly. The receptionist suddenly winked at Mike who couldn't resist looking suitably roguish. Laura was by now very keen to get away from this embarrassing scene and started to walk towards the lifts. As Mike followed, he gave her a proprietary pat on her bottom – solely for the benefit of the receptionist.

Upstairs in their room, the porter set down the cases and opened up the curtains. Mike fished in his pocket for a tip. He found a fifty-pence piece and tried to flick it casually to the porter but his aim was badly out and the coin shot straight up in the air and landed somewhere over his own head. Feeling suitably foolish, he fumbled in his pocket for another coin.

This time he played it safe and handed it over. The porter thanked him, gave him an odd look, and then left. As soon as the door had closed behind him, Mike got down on his hands and knees to look for the first coin. Laura stood by the bed, hands on hips, looking down at him.

'All right, what was that about?' she demanded.

'Well, he obviously knew,' Mike said.

Laura tapped her foot impatiently. 'I'm aware that he obviously knew. I just don't enjoy that sort of male sniggery stuff, that's all.'

'I thought it was very discreet.'

'You, I mean.'

'Oh. Well, I don't know why you should feel aggrieved. You're the one who's here on business, so what does that make me? A bit of fun for the weekend? I'm the one they'll be sniggering at, I'm the one they'll whisper about.'

She saw the funny side of this. 'Fool,' she smiled.

Mike found the missing coin and stood up. 'Ah! Now – shall I slip into something more comfortable?' he asked provocatively.

'I'd sooner you turned that muzak off,' Laura said. The strains of 'Viva España' were beginning to get to her.

'Right.' Mike sprawled across one of the twin beds in order to reach the controls of the console. After switching several lights on and off, he finally managed to put a stop to the music.

'Are you sure you're not going to be bored, Mike?' Laura said, checking through her working itinerary for the weekend.

'Me? No.'

'It's a pretty intensive schedule, you see. Nearly all day tomorrow, then half a day Sunday.'

'You don't have to eat with them, do you?'

'Oh, no.'

'Well, then. I'll see you for meals – see you in the evenings – nights.'

'You're making this sound like a dirty weekend.'

'Well, it doesn't have to be totally clean, does it?'

Laura smiled at him. 'I'm glad you came,' she said.

There was a knock on the door and a waiter entered. 'You rang for service, sir?' he enquired.

Mike looked puzzled. 'No,' he replied.

The waiter indicated the console. 'Are you sure, sir?'

Mike looked across at the console and noticed a tell-tale red light.

'Oh – rang,' he said guiltily. 'Yes, I did. Sorry, I did ring.'

There was a pause, and the waiter looked confused. 'Is there something I can get you, sir?' he finally asked.

Mike considered this for a moment or two, then, believing himself to be on fairly safe ground, said: 'I don't suppose you could get hold of a bottle of very good champagne at this hour of the afternoon, could you?'

'Certainly, sir,' the waiter said deferentially.

'Oh. Fine,' Mike said, unhappily.

After the waiter had scurried away to fetch the champagne, Laura turned to Mike and pointed out, 'You could have simply told him you pressed the wrong button.'

'Yes, I know, but we've already dropped one clanger. We don't want to get a reputation for it, do we?'

'I wonder how much a bottle of very good champagne costs?' Laura mused.

There was that to consider, of course. 'I'll do something cheap tomorrow,' Mike promised.

Laura smiled grimly. 'You may have to.'

*

The following morning after a walk – or rather a hobble – along the beach, Mike thought he'd pass a pleasant half-hour or so amusing himself on the Crazy Golf course. The first hole was straightforward enough but the second was proving difficult. The idea was to get the ball through the door of a little house, round the gully inside and then out of the back door where it should, preferably, end up near the hole. Mike struck the ball confidently and watched it shoot neatly into the little house. He was just about to walk round the other side when it rolled back out again – the way it had entered. Painstakingly, Mike placed the ball for another shot, aware by this time that he had collected an audience – a solemn little boy with glasses who was watching him owlishly. Mike hit the ball once more and it disappeared inside the house, paused and then rolled back out again. The owl sidled up in order to get a better view. Self-consciously, Mike tried again, this time giving the ball a firmer tap. The ball went into the little house. There was a longer and more significant pause and Mike was convinced he'd cracked it. He hadn't. The ball reappeared and rolled relentlessly back towards his feet. He sighed and handed his putter to the little boy. The budding Ballesteros hit the ball firmly and expertly. It rolled into the house and shot out the other side before plopping neatly in the hole. The little boy allowed himself a smile of satisfaction before handing the putter back to Mike. It was a childish game anyway, Mike thought, as he called it a day and walked off the course.

After a brisk and chilly walk around the floral gardens, Mike decided to return to the hotel and wait in the bar for Laura. It was still rather early and the place was deserted except for a couple of men sitting at a table and chatting quietly. As he approached the bar Mike noticed that the barman was the waiter from whom he had ordered the expensive bottle of champagne the previous day.

'Good morning, sir,' the waiter said, recognizing the big spender instantly. 'Did you enjoy the champagne yesterday?'

'Yes, very much,' Mike said, trying to give the impression that it wasn't anything out of the ordinary for him to be sipping vintage champagne in the afternoon.

'What'll it be today, sir?'

For a wild moment, Mike considered ordering something exotic. Thinking better of it, he said, 'Half of bitter, please.' He looked idly round the bar and nodded politely to the only other occupants – the two men. The waiter passed Mike his humble beer and Mike took a sip. Beginning to feel rather hungry, he looked at his watch to see how much longer Laura would be.

One of the men noticed this and said cheerily, 'About ten minutes, old man.'

'Sorry?'

'They break for lunch in about ten minutes.'

'Oh. How did you know I was waiting?'

'Experience. Veterans of a hundred seminars, aren't we, Chris?' he said, turning to his companion, who nodded sagely, and said:

'Scarred – scarred veterans.'

'Come and join us,' the first man invited.

Mike wasn't too keen on the idea, but, not wanting to seem stand-offish, he picked up his beer and went to sit with the scarred veterans at their table.

'Mike Selway,' he said, introducing himself.

'David Payne. Chris Grover,' David said.

Chris looked around the bar forlornly. 'Why do we do it?' he said.

'Do what?' Mike asked.

'Let our wives talk us into coming to these things.

They're the interpreters – it's their job – but "We'll get bored when we're not working," they say. "We'll have the evenings together," they say. And we fall for it and here we sit – off-season ghosts, wishing we were stronger-willed.'

At this juncture, Mike realized that both Chris and Dave had taken it for granted that he was also married.

'Oh, I see. Yes,' he nodded.

'Did yours wheedle?' Dave asked.

'My . . . well, actually no. I volunteered.'

The two old hands shook their heads sadly at this basic beginner's mistake.

'You can't have been married long,' David deduced, smiling sympathetically.

'No,' Mike said, beginning now to wish he'd stayed aloof.

'Why do we do it?' Chris repeated, staring moodily into his lager.

'Men of straw,' David said.

'Mike volunteered,' Chris pointed out.

Mike shuffled about in his seat. It was too late now to change his story. It was one thing lying to hotel receptionists, but maybe Chris and David would think it rather odd.

'Ah, here they come,' David said, as some of the convention members, wearing their badges, started to make their way eagerly towards the bar. David turned to Mike. 'Look here, why don't we all have lunch together – perhaps some of your marital bliss will rub off.'

Mike could have kicked himself. He knew that he'd idiotically lied himself into a tight corner. Just then he spotted Laura, who had entered the bar and was looking around for him among the sea of thirsty conference members. He jumped up quickly. 'No thanks. We'd love to, but we're going somewhere.

Out,' he said, keeping it deliberately vague in case they should invite themselves along.

Laura had seen him by now and was making her way towards his table. Mike strode over to her and, taking her firmly by the elbow, propelled her out of the bar. They reached their room in thirty seconds flat, both badly out of breath.

As soon as they were inside their room, Laura snatched her arm away. 'Will you stop bundling me about?' she complained. 'I don't want to get my coat and I don't want to go out and eat.'

'The fresh air will do you good.'

'It's blowing a gale. The fresh air will probably blow us both into the sea. What's so wrong eating here?'

'It's very expensive,' Mike lied.

'My lunch is already paid for.'

He quickly changed tack. 'I don't think the food's that good.'

'You said the breakfast was delicious.'

'Yes, but that was breakfast. That doesn't mean to say they won't serve an awful lunch.' He was beginning to flounder and knew it. He opted for action: he crossed to the wardrobe, took out Laura's coat and started to force her into it. 'Now come on – get your coat on.'

'I will not get my coat on!' she said, and, shrugging herself loose, she sat on the bed, her arms folded grimly across her chest.

Mike knew he was beaten. He threw the coat on the other bed and sat down beside her. 'Oh, what's the use!'

'Mike, what *is* the matter with you?'

'All right. Well, I got chatting to a couple of blokes in the bar who are married to two of the girls who are interpreting here and they somehow assumed I was as well.'

She looked at him severely. 'And you somehow didn't tell them otherwise?'

'Well, there's no need to go around shouting it from the roof-tops, is there?'

'I didn't mention roof-tops.'

'Or I could drive up and down the prom with a loudspeaker on top of the van,' he said, beginning to get silly.

'All I'm saying, Mike, is, if the subject comes up, why pretend?'

That was rich, he thought. He couldn't resist this one. 'Like booking us in as Mr and Mrs Selway,' he remarked.

'That was different,' she said huffily.

'I thought it might be.' You really couldn't win.

'Well it was. I booked us in as Mr and Mrs to avoid any . . . complications.'

'That's why I went along with these blokes – to avoid complications.'

'Which is why we're stuck up here instead of having lunch in the dining-room like normal people.'

They sat in silence, morosely staring at their reflections in the wardrobe mirror.

'This whole thing is turning into a farce, isn't it?' Mike said. He got up, crossed to the wardrobe and looked carefully inside. 'No.'

'No what?'

'Well, the way things are going there should be a vicar or a French maid in there. Why doesn't anything go in a straight line for us? Everything is loops and jumbles and messes.'

'Oh, cheer up. I don't suppose our exact relationship is vitally interesting to that many people, anyway. Look, we'll have lunch up here – quite cosy, really – and, from now on, if anyone wants to know we just tell the truth. How about that?'

This pep talk seemed to make a difference

somehow, and Mike started to cheer up. 'Why not?' he said.

'Good.'

Laura picked up the telephone by the bed. 'Room service, please. No, I don't know which button to press. Thank you. Room service? This is Mr Selway's mistress in Room 504. Do you think we could have lunch in our room?' Confidently, she replaced the receiver.

Mike couldn't believe his ears. He stared at her in exasperation. He could just picture the scene in the kitchens – they'd be having a field day. In fact, they were probably tossing a coin to see who would be the lucky one to serve them the meal. For a moment, he seriously considered hiding in the wardrobe.

The next morning, Mike found himself back on the Crazy Golf course. Like a true golfer, he was determined not to let the old 'Devil Hole' beat him. With practised expertise he struck the ball. With practised expertise the ball rolled into the house and straight back out again – to land at Mike's feet. Mike looked around – luckily the would-be Ballesteros was not there to witness his humiliation a second day running. One more go, he thought. This time the ball seemed to stay inside the little house for much longer and, believing he had cracked it, Mike marched victoriously round to the other side, swinging his club nonchalantly. The ball was nowhere to be seen. Puzzled, he returned to the front of the house. No sign of it. Presumably it was stuck inside. Mike looked around once more to see if anyone was watching and then gave the house a sharp kick. Nothing. Another kick landed on the little whitewashed walls. Nothing. Mike decided the time had come to retire for good. He walked away. Behind him, his ball rolled out on the right side of the house and plopped neatly into the hole. Unaware of this hole in one, Mike continued his long walk back to the clubhouse.

By the time he reached the hotel, he was in a foul mood. He needed a drink and decided to venture into the bar. It was with some considerable relief that he saw the two world-weary conference veterans, Chris and David, were not in evidence. He ordered half a bitter from the barman, who looked at his watch and said, 'You've got about half an hour if you're waiting for your lady, sir.'

It was a perfectly innocent remark but Mike was, by this time, highly sensitive when it came to the subject of mistresses, wives and girlfriends. He glared at the barman. 'What's that supposed to mean?' he asked, instantly hostile.

'The seminar, sir. The afternoon session has got about half an hour to go.'

'Not that. What's this "your lady" supposed to mean?'

The barman shrugged. 'Just an expression.'

'Why use it on me?'

'I'm sorry, sir,' he apologized. 'I always say it.'

'Well, it's a damn silly thing to say.'

The barman looked hurt. 'I beg your pardon,' he said stiffly. 'I'll say "wife" in future, sir.'

'Look, it's not really any of your business, is it?' Mike said, and turned away. His day was complete when he saw David and Chris walking into the bar.

'Hello there,' David said, spotting him immediately. 'Mind if we join you?'

'No.' Mike was beginning to regret his rather churlish attitude towards the barman and he turned to him. 'Look, I'm sorry about that. It wasn't really fair.'

'That's all right, sir.' He smiled magnanimously.

'What was all that about?' David enquired, sitting down beside Mike.

'That? Oh just . . . nothing, really.'

'Getting to you, is it?' Chris sympathized. 'Still, so long as you don't start hallucinating.'

'Did you find anywhere decent open for lunch, by the way? I've never been able to,' David said.

'No. We decided to eat in our room in the end.'

'Good Lord!' David said. 'How very romantic! You don't write books like "How to Keep Your Marriage Fresh", do you?'

Mike decided it was time to bite on the bullet. 'Laura and I aren't married,' he said apologetically.

'Oh.'

'I should have said,' Mike mumbled, looking fixedly into his beer.

'Jan and I aren't married, either,' David admitted.

Mike looked up. 'But you said . . .'

'I know. Nonconformists trying to conform.'

Mike turned to Chris. 'What about you?'

'Me. Oh yes, I'm married. I'm married all right.' He paused and then added: 'Not to the girl I'm here with, though.'

The afternoon session had finished early and Laura was looking for Mike. She stopped at the desk to ask the receptionist. 'Excuse me. Have you seen my . . .' she began, and then realized it was the same receptionist who had booked them both in. 'Mr Selway?' she said, beginning to feel herself blushing.

'I'm sorry, madam, I haven't.'

'Never mind,' she said, backing away.

A handsome, middle-aged man who had been standing nearby had reacted positively to the sound of her voice and, as she turned away from the desk, he approached her confidently. 'Excuse me, but I heard you speaking,' he said in perfect English only slightly tinged with a French accent.

Instantly jumping to the conclusion that she was being accosted by some sex freak, Laura backed away. 'What do you mean?' she asked suspiciously. 'I don't know what you're talking about. What do you mean?'

The handsome stranger smiled down at her. 'Your voice. It is the voice that has been talking into my ear in the conference.'

'Oh, I see. Yes,' Laura said, relaxing her attitude.

'A very attractive voice,' the Frenchman said, his deep blue eyes holding hers in a hypnotic stare.

Laura blushed. 'Thank you.'

'Could I ask you a small favour? Would you say "*peut-être*" for me?'

She looked around the crowded lobby. 'What, now?'

'Please.' He smiled. It was an irresistible smile.

'It seems a bit silly,' she said, hesitating. She gave in. 'All right. *Peut-être* – there you are.'

'Ah!' he said, with a deep sigh. 'You know, I have imagined during those very boring speeches how your lips would form the word. They form it beautifully.'

This unexpected and unlooked-for compliment made Laura acutely aware of her lips.

'Would you favour me further by saying "*produit*"?' he begged.

Laura immediately started to comply but then something odd struck her. 'Just a minute. Why have I been translating English into French for you?' she asked suspiciously. 'You speak English perfectly.'

He was completely unabashed at this accusation. 'Oh, these conferences,' he shrugged, as only the French know how to, 'they can be very tiresome. I prefer to close my eyes and listen to the voice in my ear.' Laura found herself closing her eyes dreamily but stopped herself just in time. 'To imagine the lips forming the words – the face that encircles the lips, the body . . .'

Somehow she was aware only of this man and, as though in a trance, she felt herself drawn instinctively towards him, her lips . . . Someone pushed past and she realized just where she was and who she was. 'I don't think we should go on with this,' she said weakly.

'But why not, Miss' – he looked at her badge – 'Dalton.'

'It's Mrs – Mrs Dalton,' she said quickly and firmly.

'Miss Dalton!' the receptionist called out to her.

'Yes?' Laura responded, giving herself away without thinking.

'I've just been told that Mr Selway is in the bar.'

'Thank you,' she said foolishly.

The Frenchman smiled regretfully. Feeling very much like a silly schoolgirl, Laura quickly turned on her heels and walked away, not even daring to look over her shoulder.

As she entered the bar, her heart still beating wildly, she saw with some dismay that Mike was engrossed in amiable conversation with David and Chris and their two female companions. Laura tried, unsuccessfully, to attract Mike's attention. Noticing her urgent signals, the barman stepped forward

'Can I help you, madam?' he asked.

'Yes. Could you ask' – she covered her badge with her hand before continuing – 'Mr Selway to come over, please?'

'Yes, of course,' the barman said, and turned away.

Laura, who was keeping an eye on Mike, was not aware that the Frenchman had followed her into the bar. Seeing her standing alone, he approached her and spoke softly into her ear. 'And where is your Mr Selway? Is he perhaps a phantom?'

Laura jumped guiltily. 'No. He is not a phantom. He's just coming – and he's got a very nasty temper,' she added, for good measure.

Mike came towards her. He was smiling and looking not at all like a man with a very nasty temper.

'Especially when he's smiling,' Laura said quickly.

'The French have a word for this,' he said, shrugging beautifully: 'Defeat' – and he walked away.

'Hello,' Mike said. 'Who was that?'

'Nobody. Just a man who likes the way I say "*peut-être*".'

'*Peut-être*? That means "perhaps", doesn't it?'

'Yes,' she said, thinking secret thoughts.

'Perhaps to what?' Mike asked.

'I didn't say "perhaps" to anything.'

'How is it he likes the way you say it, then?' Mike asked suspiciously.

'I was interpreting for him.'

Mike glared along the bar in the Frenchman's general direction.

'There's no need to glare,' she said.

'Well, who does he think he is?'

'Casanova.'

'And who does he think you are?'

'Your mistress.'

'Oh, he does, does he?'

By this stage, they were so caught up with their discussion that they were forgetting to lower their voices, and the barman was able to hear every word.

'Well, I am your mistress,' Laura said, matter-of-factly.

'Yes. Well, I don't like the word. See over there' – and he pointed to the women sitting with Chris and David – 'they're mistresses.'

Laura had a good look. Both women were younger than her and very attractive. 'I don't know whether to feel insulted or flattered,' she said.

The barman could no longer remain silent on the subject. 'Flattered, madam. That's how I'd feel,' he said.

'Would you?' Laura asked, genuinely interested.

'Oh, yes.' He turned to Mike. 'Would your lady like a drink, sir?' he enquired politely.

Mike suddenly realized that he liked the sound of the word as well. 'Yes. Thank you. My lady would like a drink,' he said, smiling.

'Champagne?' the waiter suggested.

'Half a bitter,' Laura said.

'Worth a try,' the barman said regretfully.

'They were the ones who said they were married,' Mike said.

'Oh.'

'Do you know, I'm getting the distinct feeling that we're the only respectable couple here.'

Laura looked round the bar and then pointed out a grey-haired elderly couple sitting by the door.

'Well, almost.'

'Shall we go out to dinner tonight?' she asked.

'Well, I look at it this way. We've already blown half your pay on one bottle of good champagne. Why not blow the other half on another bottle and have dinner in our room?'

Mike was looking decidedly cheeky and Laura quickly got the message. She looked at him and smiled slowly. '*Peut-être*,' she said, relishing the pout.

6

Mike crunched on some salt-and-vinegar-flavoured crisps and tried to concentrate on a garden plan he was drawing. He was distracted by Laura who was curled up on the couch, avidly reading a glossy cookery book and murmuring the names of various dishes with some relish.

'*Escalopes à l'Orange . . . Caneton aux Cerises . . . Poussins Citronés aux Fines Herbes,*' she intoned.

'Like a crisp?' Mike asked, proffering the bag.

'No thanks.' She resumed her gastronomic incantation. '*Médaillons de Bœuf à la Russe* . . . Grilled Mackerel with Green Gooseberry Sauce.'

Mike put down his pad and pencil. 'With what?'

'Green Gooseberry Sauce.'

He pulled a face. 'You don't think all of this is going to make rather a heavy supper, do you?'

'Ha, ha. No, I'm just looking. I like looking.'

There was definitely something in her attitude that indicated something was afoot. Mike decided to give up working on his plan and went to sit down beside her. She flicked idly through the book for a few moments before she came clean.

'No, well, the thing is, Mike, I think it would be nice if we gave a dinner party.' She deliberately didn't look at him as she said this, but she could immediately sense his hostility to the suggestion.

'Why?' he demanded.

'No special reason. I'd just like to.'

'Oh.' He pulled a face.

'And I can see that you'd like to as well.'

'You know I'm not very keen on going to "dos" like that.'

'You wouldn't have to go anywhere. You'd be there already – here.'

He wasn't convinced. From past experience he knew only too well that an amazing number of things were likely to go wrong on occasions like these and, anyway, he was a creature of habit – anything that disturbed his domestic routine was to be regarded with the utmost suspicion and distrust.

'What would I have to do?' he asked doubtfully.

'Very little. Be the host – look after the drinks – keep the conversation flowing.'

A shudder went through him at this last suggestion. If there was one thing Mike couldn't do, it was make small talk. He had quite enough difficulty keeping his own conversation flowing, let alone helping other people converse.

'You don't have to do much yourself,' Laura encouraged. 'Just ask a few questions, like "So how did you get here?", and they'll tell you.'

'Biologically?'

She decided to ignore this facetious remark. 'People love telling you which route they took and then one thing leads to another and, before you know it, you've got them chatting away like mad.'

'You've done this before, haven't you?'

'Well, you must have done it some time.'

'No. I've always been the one who's been asked how I got here – and I've always been the one who bored everybody to death telling them.'

This was getting her nowhere, so Laura deliberately switched to a different kind of argument – one she knew wouldn't fail. 'It was never any fun giving dinner parties when I was on my own,' she sighed.

Mike knew he was being emotionally blackmailed

here and was powerless to prevent it. 'Now don't start that,' he said, beginning to feel himself weakening fast.

She opened her eyes wide in innocence. 'I'm not starting anything.' She knew she was winning, but couldn't resist one last, heart-tugging gesture. She looked at her cookery book, sighed pathetically, closed it and put it aside. Mike was a lost man.

'Well, I don't fancy that mackerel with the green gooseberry sauce,' he said.

She smiled, a half-guilty victory smile. 'Who shall we ask?' she said, picking up a piece of paper and a pencil.

Beginning to wonder just what he'd let himself in for, Mike asked suspiciously, 'How many people do you want?'

'I thought us and four guests.'

'Well, Phil and Helen,' he said, feeling on safe ground here.

'Yes, we must ask Phil and Helen,' she said. He noticed a slight hesitation on her part.

'I like Phil and Helen,' he said firmly.

'It's rather unimaginative, I suppose, asking your own sister, but we've had a lot of meals at their place.'

'Anyway, they're nice people. We must ask them.' No matter what, he wasn't going to see his only allies left off the list.

'Right,' Laura said, putting their names at the top of the paper. 'So that's Phil and Helen for a start.'

'Right,' Mike said, feeling happier about the situation now.

They both considered who else they might ask. On reflection they didn't seem to be spoiled for choice and a long list of suitable guests didn't exactly spring to mind.

'We must know somebody else,' Mike said, after a long pause.

'Not couples. You never really know many couples until you're a couple.'

'Well, we are – more or less.'

'Not for long enough, maybe?'

'Yes, that must be it,' Mike said, although he wasn't at all convinced that this was the real reason.

'I'll ring Helen on the morning. I hope they can come.'

'It's beginning to look essential.'

Determined to get things moving before Mike had second thoughts about the whole enterprise, Laura phoned Helen the following morning. As far as Laura's dinner parties were concerned, Helen now considered herself to be something of a hardened veteran and, when Laura eagerly reeled off the menu she had planned, she had slight misgivings.

'You're not being a little ambitious, are you?' she asked, choosing her words with care. There were loud protests at the other end of the line and Helen was accused outright of being a killjoy. 'I just think that, with dinner parties, it's best to do something that you've cooked before,' Helen insisted gently. There was an immediate and sarcastic response to this. 'No, not egg and chips!' Helen said. It was no good, Laura would have to find out the hard way – and she undoubtedly would. 'All right, you're the hostess,' she conceded. 'Friday, then – about eight.'

She hung up and wondered how she'd break the news to Phil, who was difinitely not one of Laura's culinary fans. She'd have to make it up to him the following day by cooking one of his favourite meals. Feeling happier, she returned with some relish to her mid-morning snack – ice cream, Marmite and cream crackers.

*

After phoning Helen, Laura went through her address book for the third time. At first glance, it seemed to be packed full of names, but a closer inspection revealed the usual boring information about dentists, doctors, local restaurants and – always a good standby – Paddington Station Enquiries. Finally, she settled for Jill Haynes, a woman she knew only slightly through her job as interpreter.

It was a difficult, not to say embarrassing, phone call to make because Jill Haynes obviously didn't remember her straight away. 'We met at a Trade Conference in Bournemouth last year,' Laura said, beginning to feel hot and bothered. 'Interpreting, Laura Dalton.' This didn't ring any bells either and she was forced to describe herself: 'Oh, shortish, fair, quite attractive . . . Yes, that's it. I got stuck in the lift. Hello again . . . Look, Jill, we said we'd ring, so I thought it would be nice if you and . . . your chap . . . Frank, that's it . . . came to dinner . . . You will? Oh, good . . . No, look, I'll pop a little map in the post . . . Look forward to seeing you, then. Oh, by the way, do you and Frank have any particular hates in the eating lines? . . . No, I *meant* in the vegetarian line . . . Oh, good. See you Friday, then . . . Yes. 'Bye.'

She hung up. Trust her to pick a vegetarian to invite round for dinner. She'd have to replan her whole menu now to include some meatless dishes. Feverishly she flicked through her cookery book.

On D-Day – Dinner Party Day – Laura was up at the crack of dawn hoovering and cleaning as if there were no tomorrow. Mike, disturbed by the upheaval in the living-room, decided to get dressed and investigate.

'What time do you call this?' he said, raising his voice above the noise of the hoover.

'Pardon?'

'I said, What time do you call this?'

'You sound like Charlie.'

'What?'

'I said, I'm hoovering.'

'Why?'

'Pardon?' she said, making a big production of hoovering around his feet.

Mike remained firmly rooted to the spot, and she reluctantly switched off the machine.

'I said, Why are you hoovering at this time in the morning?'

'Because it's our dinner party tonight.'

'That's ten hours away!' he pointed out.

'There's lots to do. Now have you seen any napkin rings knocking about?'

'I've just got out of bed!'

'Not this morning – knocking about generally. I'm sure I had some.'

'They must be somewhere,' Mike said, standing in the middle of the room and looking around vaguely at eye-level as though he fully expected to see them materialize in mid-air.

'Well, could you look?' Laura demanded, irritated by his unhelpful presence.

'Where?' he asked, still standing uselessly in the middle of the room.

'If I knew where, I wouldn't be asking you to look, would I?'

Mike sighed loudly. He might just as well wave goodbye to a quiet, leisurely breakfast. He started to look in a drawer in a desultory fashion.

Laura watched him and fumed inwardly. 'Oh, don't bother. I'll buy some,' she said, elbowing him out of the way.

'Why spend money buying napkin rings when you've got napkin rings?'

'Because you can't find them,' she snapped, writing on a list which was already fairly extensive. 'Six napkin rings,' she said.

Mike looked over her shoulder and did a double-take when he saw the list. 'Have you *got* to get all that stuff?'

'Yes.'

'For six people?'

'You don't realize.'

'No,' he said, looking again. 'What do we want six new dinner plates for? We've got dinner plates.'

'They don't match,' Laura pointed out. Men knew nothing when it came to such things.

'What's a *bain-marie*?'

'A kind of saucepan.'

'I don't know. Things to cook the food in. Things to serve the food on. You will be getting some food, will you?'

'Oh, don't try to be funny, Mike, please!' Laura said, beginning to feel very flustered now. 'I've got two meals to think about.'

'Two?'

'Jill and Frank are vegetarians.'

'Oh well, that's no problem. Give them what we're having without the meat.'

She glared at him. 'We're having casserole. What do you suggest I do – give them a plate of gravy each?'

He saw the dilemma. He took another look at the list. 'You don't need five different sorts of cheeses,' he said, hoping to simplify matters for her.

'Will you go away and leave me to it – please.'

'What's a ramekin?'

'Go to work!' she ordered, pushing him bodily out of the room.

'What about breakfast?'

'Oh, you can forget breakfast. I've got no time to cook breakfast.'

He knew he'd made a grave mistake by agreeing to go along with this dinner party idea. 'I'm glad we don't do this more often,' he said over his shoulder, as he walked towards the kitchen. He opened the door and stopped in his tracks. 'Hells bells!' he said, looking around incredulously.

'What?' Laura said in alarm, thinking perhaps the kitchen was on fire.

'It looks as though it's been hit by a bomb!' To Mike's eyes it seemed that every available cooking utensil, dish and bowl had been put out, filling every available surface. There were even dishes on the floor.

'I'm getting prepared,' Laura explained.

'What for? A state banquet?'

'I wish you'd go to work.'

'Well, I mean to say,' he grumbled.

'What? What do you mean to say?' She squared up to him. By this time she was just about ready for a row.

'It's just a little dinner party. Bit of food, bit of wine . . .'

'Drop,' she corrected.

'Drop. But you're turning it into an epic.'

'I just want it to be right. Surely you can understand that?'

'I can, but if you're in this sort of flap at eight o'clock in the morning, what are you going to be like tonight?'

'Organized, poised and calm,' she said with dignity.

'That sounds like a theory.'

'It *is* a theory,' she admitted.

Mike wandered around the battlefield. 'I don't suppose I'm allowed in there to make myself some breakfast?'

'No.'

'I'll get some on my way to work.'

'Try to get home early, will you?'

'Why?'

'To help.'

'I don't have a dinner suit.'

She gave him a warning look. 'I know,' he said, giving up. 'You just want it to be right.'

'Yes.'

'Well, it will be. If in any way effort equals results, it will be wonderful.'

'You're just saying that,' she said, looking worried.

'I'll be off now.'

'All right. You will . . .'

'Yes, I'll be home early,' he promised. 'See you later.' They kissed goodbye. Mike opened the front door and then paused. 'Those napkin rings,' he said thoughtfully. 'Are they wooden with a sort of carved flower on top?'

'Yes.'

'I have seen them.'

'Where?' she asked, brightening up.

'I can't remember,' he said, and made a quick exit.

Laura finished her housework in record time and then rushed out to do the shopping. To get everything on the list was a mammoth feat of endurance, comparable only to an army assault course. The shops were crowded but she made it with time to spare and by lunchtime was loaded to the gunwales with kitchen accessories and foods of every description. Loaded as she was with four carrier bags, she decided to treat herself to a taxi, but it was on the way back to the flat that she realized she had forgotten to tell Mike to get the drinks. It was only a short diversion to his office, and she directed the driver to Selway Land-scape Gardening.

As the taxi approached the yard, she noticed an ambulance drawn up outside, its blue light flashing. She immediately jumped to the conclusion that Mike had had some terrible accident and, telling the driver to wait, she rushed across the road. It was with considerable relief that she saw Mike standing on the pavement talking to one of the ambulancemen. Somebody was being carried on a stretcher up to the ambulance.

As soon as Mike saw Laura he went up to her. 'It's Charlie,' he said, looking pale and shocked. 'He collapsed. I'm going to the hospital with him.'

'I'm coming too,' Laura said, and started to climb into the back of the ambulance.

The taxi driver leaned out of his cab. 'Oy! Am I waiting in vain here, or what?' he demanded.

'Just a minute!' Mike yelled.

'My meter's still ticking!' the driver yelled back. The ultimate threat.

Mike crossed over the road to him. 'You're all heart you, aren't you? How much do we owe you?'

'Four fifty. Call it a fiver.'

'No, I'll call it four fifty,' Mike said and paid him off.

Laura called out from the back of the ambulance. 'Come on, Mike! They want to go!'

'All right,' Mike said, and ran across the road.

The driver of the cab yelled after him sarcastically, 'Have a nice day!'

'And you!' Mike shouted as the taxi pulled away. He started to climb into the back of the ambulance, when Laura made a discovery.

'Oh, Mike, I've left the shopping in the taxi.'

Luckily, the ambulance was going the same way as the taxi and they quickly overhauled it. While the ambulance waited, Mike and Laura clambered out, charged over to the taxi and retrieved the shopping. They dashed back to the ambulance and jumped in. As the doors closed and the ambulance pulled away, several Maris Piper potatoes and a few choice English tomatoes bumped down the steps and on to the road.

Laura sat down to wait in the endless grey hospital corridor. There was a constant flow of people walking purposefully backwards and forwards. Every time anyone who looked even vaguely official walked past, Laura looked to them hopefully for news, but it was as if she didn't exist. They appeared totally at ease and relaxed in their clinical environment, and Laura supposed that they had long since stopped paying attention to distraught visitors. Minutes passed like hours. An elderly patient in a dressing-gown and slippers – presumably a trusty from the geriatric ward – shuffled past slowly, singing 'Rock of Ages'. This cheered Laura up immensely and she was relieved when Mike rejoined her.

'I phoned Charlie's sister,' he said, sitting down beside her.

'Is she coming?'

'No. She said with her leg she can't even get past the front gate.' In any other situation the sheer lunacy of this statement might have raised a smile but they were too shocked to react now.

'That leaves us.'

'Yes. Any news?'

'No. Everybody just walks past.' She checked her watch. 'I should have started cooking by now.'

'But we don't know what's going to happen, do we? We're going to have to call it off.'

'We can't. Jill's at work somewhere and I don't know her number.'

Mike did some quick lateral thinking. 'I know. Ring Helen and ask her to go round to the flat and start cooking.'

Laura indicated the carrier bags, bulging with food, at her feet. 'The food is here.'

'Oh yes.'

'Wait, though. If Helen could come here, collect the food and the key, go back to the flat –'

'No,' Mike interrupted. 'No. You can't make guests cook their own dinner. Look, there's no point in us both staying. You go back.'

'No.' She was adamant about this. 'Charlie's all on his own.'

Touched by her concern, Mike kissed her gently on the cheek. She took hold of his hand and gave it a squeeze. A few more minutes ticked slowly by. Mike looked around. He felt so helpless. 'I wish somebody would come,' he sighed.

'So do I.'

He glanced down idly at one of the carrier bags and noticed some peas sticking out of the top. 'Are they for tonight?' he asked.

'Yes.' She watched in amazement as Mike got up, crossed to a nearby trolley, picked up a kidney dish, secreted it under his jacket and then sat down again. 'What are you doing?'

'Well, we might as well do something,' he said. He balanced the dish carefully on his lap and started shelling peas into it.

Laura looked around guiltily, expecting to see an irate staff nurse bearing down on them at any moment. No one was taking the slightest bit of notice, so she joined in with careless abandon.

By the time they got back to the flat, it was gone seven o'clock. Laura hurled herself into the kitchen like a ferret down a rabbit hole, and within ten minutes the place was a complete and utter shambles as she set about doing ten different things at once, finishing none of them. Mike found himself dragged along helplessly in her slipstream, and for a mad five minutes he tried to get changed and lay the table at the same time.

Laura dashed off to the bedroom to change, and left him to supervise the cooking. He noticed that the casserole was bubbling away furiously on top of the oven. 'There's something boiling here!' he called out.

'Well, turn it down, then!' Laura yelled.

He looked at the oven controls. 'Where to?'

'Just down,' came back the the irritated reply.

He adjusted the heat but without any real confidence that he'd done the right thing. Having organized the main course to the best of his ability, he looked around for something else to do and noticed the peas, still standing in the kidney dish.

'Shall I start the peas?' he called.

'No,' came the reply. 'The meat takes three hours.'

He looked at his watch and worked out that, at this rate, it wasn't so much a case of a late dinner as an early breakfast. Laura re-entered the kitchen at high speed, wearing a long evening dress and looking extremely hot and flustered.

'We shan't be eating till about eleven,' she said fretfully. She noticed that the meat had stopped cooking altogether. 'Not that far down,' she said, and quickly altered the controls.

'I've peeled some potatoes,' Mike said.

'We're having jacket potatoes!' she wailed hysterically.

'Well, shall I stick the peel back on?' Mike joked.

'Sorry, Mike,' she said, making a big effort to calm down. 'Where did I put my pinny?'

'I don't know.' He picked up the dress Laura was

wearing at the hospital and which she had thrown hastily into the corner. 'You said, "I've got to get changed", and took your dress off. Then you said, "No, I'd better start the meat", so you put your pinny on and . . .'

Laura, who had been following this retracing of her steps, suddenly realized something. She reached up under the dress she was wearing, fiddled about and then produced the pinny.

'You're panicking, aren't you?' Mike said.

'Yes,' she admitted.

'I'll finish laying the table,' he offered, and picked up a handful of cutlery.

'Are you sure that you don't want to ring the hospital?'

'They said in the morning. Anyway, they've got our number.'

'They might have let us see him.'

'Still "resting comfortably". They always say that, don't they?'

Mike had a brief mental picture of Charlie stretched out on a bed, dressed completely in white hospital clothes, except for his cap. 'Poor old Charlie,' he said.

'He'll be all right,' Laura said, trying to be optimistic but beginning to feel decidedly depressed.

'Yes. Tough as old boots,' Mike said.

This reminded Laura of something and she looked at the meat bubbling away in the casserole. 'Please be tender, please,' she whispered.

Mike overheard this. 'What do you mean?' he asked.

'I was talking to the meat.'

The doorbell rang and she jumped. 'Somebody's arrived,' Mike said, frozen to the floor.

'Well, somebody's supposed to, aren't they?'

'Don't get ratty.'

'Sorry. I just want it all to be so perfect,' she said, looking around at the chaos.

'It will be – just a bit late, that's all.'

Still clutching a handful of knives and forks, Mike went reluctantly to open the door and admit the unsuspecting dinner guests. When he opened the door, he found himself confronted by all four guests at once. Jill, Frank, Phil and Helen had met on the way up to the flat and were now all chatting away quite happily as if they'd known one another for years.

'Ah!' Mike said. 'It's everybody.'

'Well, we all found ourselves coming to the same flat, so we thought we must be,' Phil said.

'Come in, come in. Hello, I'm Mike,' Mike said, to no one in particular.

'Hello, I'm Phil,' Phil said, shaking him by the hand.

Jill and Frank laughed at this but Mike was too nervous to respond to the joke. Helen sensed immediately that Mike was in a state of shock and made the introductions on his behalf. They filtered through to the living-room and Mike stood by the table, still holding on to the cutlery.

'I must say, you were easy to find,' Frank said.

'What? Oh, good,' Mike mumbled as he realized he'd missed his opening gambit. He remembered Laura's advice and asked the magic question: 'How *did* you get here?'

'We drove,' Frank said.

'Oh,' Mike said, not expecting such a short answer. 'Well, do all sit down,' he added, waving the cutlery about in the air.

'Well, this is all very nice, isn't it?' Helen said.

'Yes, jolly nice,' Frank agreed.

'Jolly nice,' Jill echoed.

There was an awkward silence. Mike knew it was

his job as host to get the conversational ball rolling again.

'We were easy . . .' he started, but Phil chipped in at the same time with a question and they both broke off in mid-sentence.

'Sorry, go on,' Mike said.

Helen gave Phil a small negative signal.

'No, you carry on, Mike,' Phil said. 'What were you saying?'

'Well, I was only saying to . . . er . . .?'

'Frank,' Frank reminded him.

'Frank – that we were easy to find, then?'

This set things back somewhat.

'Yes. Very easy, actually,' Frank answered, not quite knowing how he could elaborate on this.

'It only took just under an hour from Chorleywood,' Jill added.

'Really?' Phil said politely.

'Of course, it's quicker in the evenings,' Jill remarked.

'The traffic is lighter then, isn't it?' Phil said.

'Yes, it is,' she agreed.

'Or early in the morning,' Mike said, thinking that maybe he should contribute something.

'What?' said Frank, confused.

'The traffic,' Mike explained.

'Oh, yes. It *is* lighter early in the mornings,' Frank said.

Mike had now run out of things to say about the traffic and looked anxiously towards the kitchen, hoping for reinforcements.

'Shall I give Laura a hand?' Helen asked.

'Oh, no. She'll be out in a minute,' Mike said, but without any real hope of seeing her put in an appearance much before midnight.

'Good. I'm starving,' Phil said.

'So am I. I could eat a horse,' Mike laughed, and

then remembered that two of his guests were vegetarians and might find this colloquialism in bad taste. He looked across at them guiltily, but they were pretending they hadn't heard.

Laura made her entrance from the kitchen, surrounded by clouds of steam. She was making a considerable effort to appear the perfect unruffled hostess. 'Sorry. One or two little things to do,' she announced lightly.

Helen instantly recognized all the signs of a cooking disaster in the making. 'Are you sure you don't want a hand?' she asked.

'No, there's no rush,' Laura said quickly, not wanting her sister to witness the extent of the débâcle. 'Hello, Phil.'

'Hi.'

'Jill, how nice to see you again.'

'You too. Sorry I didn't remember you at first. Laura, this is Frank.'

'Hello,' Frank said.

'I'm so glad you could come. How did you get here?'

Jill and Frank exchanged glances. 'Oh, we drove,' Frank said.

Jill was now word-perfect and added: 'It only took us about fifty minutes.'

'That's from Chorleywood,' Frank said, joining in with the familiar refrain.

'Oh, that's good, isn't it? Isn't that good?' Laura said nervously.

Phil didn't particularly want to travel down this road again and he quickly changed the subject. 'I hope there's plenty to eat. We're all starving.'

'Good,' Laura lied. 'It will only be a couple of hours.' She knew it would be three hours at the most, but was hoping that the extra sixty minutes or so wouldn't be noticed by that stage.

This obviously came as something of a shock to everyone.

'Well, I think that's a good idea,' Helen said, trying to ease the situation for her sister. 'I can't bear going somewhere and sitting straight down to eat. It's much more civilized to have a chat first.'

Laura gave her a grateful smile. 'That's what we thought, didn't we, Mike?' she said.

'What? Yes.'

'Mike, you haven't given anybody a drink,' Laura chided.

'Oh, my goodness! Sorry! We were chatting about traffic and so on. What would you all like?'

'Oh . . . um . . . a dry sherry would be nice,' Jill said.

'Fine. Helen?'

'Gin and tonic, please, Mike.'

'Me too,' Phil said.

'Two gins and tonics. Frank?'

'May I have a small Scotch?'

'Yes, of course. One dry sherry, two gins and tonics and one Scotch coming up!' Mike said efficiently. He put down the cutlery and crossed to the drinks table. He was halfway across the room when he froze. There was a half-empty bottle of wine standing on the table. In the rush to get back from the hospital they'd forgotten to buy the drinks. 'Shan't be a minute. I've just got to tear round to the off-licence,' he said casually as he sauntered across to the front door. As soon as he reached the door, he whipped it open and dashed out. Laura gave everyone a brave smile.

It had been a long day and it was certainly proving to be a long night. Two hours later, everyone was sitting around clutching their drinks and casting frustrated glances towards the kitchen, where Laura had spent most of the evening checking on the meal. She came in, for what seemed like the hundredth time, and announced gaily, 'Only half an hour now.' Everyone was so weak with hunger by this time that they didn't even have the energy to buck up at this. Laura looked around at their gloomy faces and then gave up all pretence. 'Oh, this is awful. I've mucked it all up.'

Mike got up and put his arm round her shoulders comfortingly. 'It's not your fault,' he said, and turned to the others. 'It's Charlie, you see. He was taken ill at work and we had to go to the hospital with him and it took hours.'

Everyone was immediately sympathetic.

'Laura, you should have put us off,' Helen said.

'We couldn't. Now I expect you've all gone completely off the idea of eating at all.'

There was a weak and unconvincing chorus of 'not at alls' to this.

'Puts an edge on the appetite, a bit of a wait,' Phil said.

Laura cheered up a bit after hearing these polite lies.

'Poor old Charlie,' Mike said.

'What's wrong with him, Mike?' Helen asked.

'Ticker,' Mike said.

'Oh, dear.'

This was all that was needed to put a real damper on the evening.

'Funny old things, hearts,' Frank said.

'You take them for granted as long as they're working, don't you?' Laura said.

'You do. And then – pop!' Jill said.

'He's not that old, is he?' Phil enquired.

'You don't have to be that old,' Mike said.

'That's true.'

'Like a single-engined aeroplane. If the engine

fails . . .' Frank didn't finish the sentence. Everyone looked depressed.

'It could happen to any one of us,' Mike said.

The telephone rang and made everyone jump. Mike was there in a flash. 'Hello? Yes, it is. Oh dear. Yes, I know. No, it was good of you to call.' Everyone sat quietly, listening to Mike's subdued voice and prepared for the worst. 'I see. Look, I'll come right over. Right, Goodbye.' He hung up and turned to Laura. 'It's Charlie. He's worse. I'm sorry, Laura, I've got to go.'

'Of course,' she said. 'I'll come with you.' It was then that she remembered she had four ravenous guests to feed. 'Oh,' she said, looking around, and not quite sure what to do for the best.

'Shall we all go?' Phil asked.

'Don't be daft,' Helen said.

'This is terrible,' Laura moaned.

'It's just bad luck,' Jill said bravely.

Frank thought that, although it was ill timed, at least they now had the perfect excuse for leaving. 'Yes, look, we'll go,' he said, getting up.

'But the food's nearly ready,' Laura said. 'Please eat that.'

'There's plenty to drink now,' Mike pointed out.

'Yes,' Helen said. 'Look, you two go. We can dish up the food for ourselves.'

'We'll be all right. You'll probably be back before you know it,' Phil said.

Laura wasn't at all sure that she was doing the right thing. 'It's not supposed to be like this,' she protested.

'Come on,' Mike said, taking matters into his own hands and pushing her towards the door. Laura just had time to take off her pinny and hand it to Helen.

*

It was with a strange sense of unreality that Mike and Laura found themselves back in the endless grey corridor again. The place was even more depressing at night – the lights were dim and there were very few people to be seen. The hymn-singing escapee shuffled past warbling his favourite dirge. Mike watched him until he had disappeared from view.

'That wasn't the hospital ghost, was it?' he asked.

'I saw him this afternoon,' Laura said bleakly. 'He was singing that then.'

'That must cheer everybody up no end,' Mike said.

'No end. What's the time?'

'Half past twelve. We couldn't let Charlie think he was on his own.'

'Of course not.'

Mike's stomach rumbled loudly. 'I could murder some bread and treacle now,' he said.

'Why bread and treacle?'

'I don't know.'

Laura saw a young staff nurse approaching them and, fearing the worst, grabbed hold of Mike's hand. Automatically, they both got to their feet as she walked towards them.

'Mr and Mrs Selway?' she enquired.

'No, we're not –' Laura started to correct her but Mike realized that, in the circumstances, their relationship to each other was irrelevant.

'Yes, if you like. How is he?'

'Still in ICU but stabilized,' she said brightly.

Mike experienced a sudden flash of anger at this cold and unintelligible hospital jargon. 'What's that supposed to mean? He's a man, not a car in for service!' She looked a bit startled and Mike suddenly felt ashamed at himself for taking it out on her. 'Sorry,' he apologized.

She was sympathetic. 'No, I'm sorry,' she said, smiling at him. 'Mr Painter is still in the Intensive

Care Unit but his condition has stabilized and we think that he is out of any immediate danger.'

'Thank goodness for that,' Mike said, much relieved.

'May we see him?' Laura asked.

The nurse shook her head. 'Perhaps tomorrow. He's resting comfortably at the moment. It was very good of you to wait.'

'Well, we weren't doing anything special,' Laura said, feeling that, in the circumstances, this wasn't all that far from the truth.

'If you'd like to ring Sister in the morning, then?' the young nurse suggested.

'Yes. Give Charlie our best, won't you?' Mike said.

'Of course. Goodnight.'

They thanked her once again and watched her walk briskly back down the corridor.

'She only looked about sixteen,' Laura said.

'Oh no – seventeen.'

'I feel about one hundred and ninety.'

'I'm not surprised. We've spent most of the day tearing about like lunatics and Charlie has spent most of the day going what he normally does – resting comfortably. Well, come on. We've got your dinner party to get back to.'

They started the long walk down the corridor.

'They've probably all gone home by now.' Laura said.

'I hope they washed up.'

Mike suddenly remembered something. 'Just a minute,' he said, and took a bag from his coat pocket. Out of the bag he produced the clean kidney dish and, looking around to make sure that no one was watching, he replaced it carefully on a trolley.

*

Physically and emotionally exhausted, Mike and Laura arrived back at the flat. As they opened the front door, they were surprised to hear loud shouts and laughter coming from the living-room. They walked in and stood at the door. Brandy glasses and coffee cups were much in evidence, and Phil, Helen, Jill and Frank were sitting round the table. In the middle of the table was a plate of uncooked peas. The four dinner guests were each holding a straw and trying to suck up peas from the plate and transfer them to individual saucers in front of them. The laughter seemed to be producing a good deal of pea dropping, and the pea dropping produced a good deal of laughter. So engrossed were they in the contest that at first no one realized Mike and Laura had returned.

It was Phil who noticed them both standing wearily by the door. 'They're back,' he announced.

'Yes, we're back,' Laura said faintly.

'How's Charlie, all right?' Helen asked.

'They think he's out of danger.'

'He's resting comfortably,' Mike added in the familiar hospital jargon.

Everyone looked relieved at this good news.

'You haven't waited dinner?' Laura asked. 'It will be ruined.'

'No,' Helen said. 'I just added the finishing touches and we ate it.'

'And I must say, Laura, it was delicious,' Jill congratulated her.

'Oh, good,' Laura said, feeling totally detached from the whole affair.

'And the wine, Mike. And the wine. If I may say so, you chose very well there,' Frank said.

Mike smiled wryly. 'I thought we'd like it.'

'Yes, smashing, all of it. *And* we washed up,' Phil said.

'Not that it was his idea,' Helen laughed, digging him playfully in the ribs.

'The great pea contest was,' he said.

'I haven't laughed so much for ages,' Jill said and then, noticing Mike and Laura's pale, drawn faces, added: 'I'm sorry. That sounds awful.'

'No, we wanted you to laugh,' Laura said.

'There's some casserole left. Would you like me to heat it up for you?' Helen offered.

'No thanks. I'm past being hungry now.'

'I could do with a brandy,' Mike said.

'Me too,' Laura said.

Mike started to cross to the drinks table but Frank intercepted him. 'No, you sit down. I'll get them. Anyone else?'

'No, actually, Frank, we really ought to be going,' Jill said.

Frank looked at his watch. 'Good Lord, is that the time? I hadn't realized.'

Phil and Helen also got up to go. 'Yes, come on, Missus,' Phil said. 'Expectant fathers should be in bed by now.'

'Oh, don't all go,' Laura begged.

'No, we really must. We just wanted to see you first,' Helen said.

Frank gave Mike and Laura a couple of stiff brandies and then fetched the coats. Suddenly everyone was on the move. There was a flurry of 'goodbye's' and 'thank you's' and the door closed behind them. For a little while the chatter could be heard as the happy guests made their way down the stairway. Mike and Laura sat on the sofa with their brandies.

'Well, I'm glad they enjoyed themselves,' Mike said.

Laura looked wistful. 'Yes.'

'It would have been awful if it had been a total washout.'

'Yes.'

'And you heard what Frank said – "A very enjoyable evening".'

'Shame we missed it.'

'Yes.'

'Still, we know the secret for the next time. Get the dinner on, then clear off and leave them to it.'

For a moment, Laura was on the brink of being upset. Mike put an arm round her shoulders. Gradually, as they sat there looking at the empty coffee cups and brandy glasses, the humour of the situation began to get to them. They smiled and, raising their glasses, they toasted each other. It had been an unforgettable evening.

7

When Laura wasn't working as an interpreter on the conference circuit and had time to spare, she frequently helped Mike out at the office by handling any outstanding paperwork. Experience had taught her to avoid organizing him too much, although at times when she saw the unprofessional way he handled his business affairs the temptation was great, and she had to bite her tongue.

Charlie's sudden illness, combined with an upsurge in work, was lately proving too much for Mike to handle on his own. Jobs accumulated and became overdue, and as Mike returned home later and later Laura began to worry for him. She knew that to catch up with the backlog of orders he would have to replace Charlie, but when she suggested this Mike dug in his heels: he wasn't going to get rid of Good Old Charlie just because he had had the misfortune to fall ill. It wouldn't be fair.

As the situation neared crisis point, Laura happened to be working at the office, sorting out the accounts, and, unwittingly, found herself acting as PR lady for Selway Landscape Gardening. The incoming phone calls became increasingly irate and she was nearing breaking-point when a Mr Miller rang up to complain.

'Three weeks late?' Laura said, trying to sound surprised. 'You're quite sure that we quoted the fourteenth as our starting date? . . . You are quite sure . . . Yes, I do understand. Would you care to hold on for just one moment. We have all our jobs and staff assignments on our computer. I'll just check.' She put the receiver down on the desk. The 'computer' was, in fact, a large, untidy pile of job sheets in a filing tray. Laura sifted through them and then grimaced as she found the one she was looking for. Clearly stamped on it in red letters was the word 'urgent'. Steeling herself, she picked up the receiver. 'Hello, Mr Miller,' she said in honeyed tones. 'Yes, I'm terribly sorry but there does seem to have been a malfunction somewhere and unfortunately . . .' She broke off, unable to keep up the ridiculous deceit any longer. She dropped the clipped, formal tone she had adopted and spoke normally. 'Look, Mr Miller. I won't lie. Mr Selway's assistant is in hospital at the moment and we got behind, but Mr Selway is doing his very best to – '

Mr Miller obviously seemed to feel that this was just another delaying tactic, and the line went dead as he hung up. Laura sighed and replaced the receiver. Angrily, she picked up the job sheet and threw it down on to the floor.

Mike dragged himself into the office, holding his aching back. 'Any tea in the pot?' he asked hopefully.

'Don't you start on me!' Laura snapped.

'All I said was, Any tea in the pot?'

'I'm just tired of being started on, that's all. People have been starting on me all day.'

'What people?'

'Customers. Or, put another way, ex-customers. We're late on every job and they're beginning to ask why. I've tried everything: lying, bluffing, cajoling, putting my cards on the table, pretending I was a wrong number, and what do I have to show for it? Two cancelled orders.'

'That's better than yesterday. We had three yesterday.'

Laura, who felt that as the front man she was bearing the brunt of all the complaints, glared balefully at him. 'What sort of attitude is that?'

'Realistic.'

'Realistic! Mike, you're doing a very good job of fiddling while Rome burns.'

Mike shrugged helplessly. 'Well, what else can I do? Charlie's still in hospital. I can hardly drag him out of his bed and put him to work, can I?'

'It's been six weeks,' Laura pointed out.

'Five and a half,' he carped, beginning to feel irritated by Laura's hounding, and wanting to score a point.

'Oh!' she said sarcastically. Of course, this made all the difference.

The telephone rang. Praying that it would be another irate customer, she offered Mike the chance of answering. As if to show her he could handle it all perfectly well, he picked up the receiver and gave her a confident smile. 'Selway Landscape Gardening,' Mike said in a business-like voice, 'Mike Selway speaking. Hello, Mr Anderson, how are you?' Laura watched the expression on his face change from quiet confidence to deep embarrassment. 'Oh. Is it as long as that? . . . No, I . . . Oh well. You see . . . Yes, but . . . Now look!'

Having said his piece, Mr Anderson hung up. Now it was three lost customers. Laura picked up the relevant job sheet and threw it down on the floor with the others. Mike sat down heavily at the desk and stared wearily at the pile of remaining job sheets.

'Come on,' Laura said quietly. 'Let's call it a day.'

'No, I can't. I've got another job to do.'

'It will be dark in half an hour. What are you planning? Floodlit gardening?'

'Sort of. The couple I'm working for have got some lights on their patio.'

'And they won't mind having dinner with someone banging about outside their french windows?'

'I'm working on the theory that they'll be so glad to see me, they wouldn't mind if I had a couple of bulldozers out there.'

'What time will you be home?' she asked, knowing it was a useless question.

'I don't know. Late. Look, you get off anyway. I don't pay you to sit here and take abusive phone calls all day.'

'You don't pay me at all. I'm a volunteer, remember?'

He looked at her closely. 'Are you going off it?'

'No. I don't really mind a bit of a crisis. I quite enjoy proving what an absolute brick I am. I just wish you'd be realistic about Charlie.'

'Well, he'll be out of hospital in a few days.'

'Oh, Mike!' she said, shaking her head in disbelief.

Not wanting to get into yet another argument about Charlie, Mike stood up and put on his coat. 'I'd better go. You never know. If I start work as they start dinner, they might take pity on me and pass out a bowl of scraps.' He left quickly.

Laura looked at her watch and decided she might as well go home but, just as she was getting her things together, the telephone rang. She was torn between answering it or running away. Reluctantly, she picked up the receiver, and steeled herself for some abuse. 'Selway Landscape Gardening. Oh – ' It was Mr Miller again. 'Yes . . . as a matter of fact I *was* telling the truth . . . I really was . . . Yes, I suppose it does make a change these days . . . That's very kind of you to say so. Mr Miller, does this mean that you will be wanting us to do the job after all? . . . Oh, good . . . Provided it's by tomorrow at the latest? . . . Goodbye.' Feeling that her day at the office hadn't been entirely wasted, she retrieved the job sheet from the floor, picked up an 'urgent' stamp and stamped 'urgent' all over it. Satisfied, she put it back on the pile of current job sheets and went home.

Mike was very late home that night. Dirty, tired and still wearing his wellington boots, he staggered into the living-room where Laura was nodding off in front of the television.

'You look whacked,' she said, getting up to give him a kiss.

'No, I'm fine,' Mike protested feebly.

She turned off the television. 'Did you get your plate of scraps?' she asked.

'No – a glass of water. And they're expecting me to knock something off the bill for using their patio lights.' He collapsed with a sign into an armchair.

'Supper's only got to be heated up,' Laura said, and went towards the kitchen.

'You shouldn't have waited up for me.'

'I don't mind.'

Making a huge effort, he sat up and tried to pull off his wellington boots, but it was an unequal struggle and he subsided back into the chair. Laura stood for a while, looking at him, then she crossed over and, kneeling down in front of him, eased off his boots.

'Come on, oh Sultan!' she said, and he smiled gratefully. 'Oh, Mr Miller phoned back. We've still got the job,' she said, giving him the good news first. 'If we can do it tomorrow,' she added.

'It *is* tomorrow, isn't it?'

'I didn't mean to be a nag about Charlie,' she apologized.

'I put that down to combat fatigue.'

'I just wish you'd be realistic,' she said.

'I promised to keep the job open for him.'

'Till when?'

'Till he's better.'

'Mike, he's an old man who's had a fairly severe heart attack. He isn't going to get better – not properly better.'

'Have you ever thought of taking up hospital visiting? You'd be a real tonic for the patients.'

'You've got to face facts,' she said, trying to keep the rising irritation out of her voice, but failing.

'He's as tough as old boots, Charlie.'

'Even old boots wear out.'

'He's got to be given a chance,' Mike insisted.

'To do what? His normal speed was dead slow. If he ever makes it back to work, he'll simply grind to a complete halt.'

Every bone in his body ached and he was feeling much too exhausted to argue with Laura. Deep in the back of his mind he knew she was right, but he couldn't face up to the problem now. 'Is the supper ready yet?' he asked, deliberately changing the subject. Laura shrugged hopelessly and got up to go to the kitchen.

'Mules? They're not in it!' she said softly – but just loud enough for Mike to hear.

While Laura was out of the room, Mike made the mistake of leaning back in his chair and closing his eyes for a second. Sleep claimed him almost immediately and by the time Laura came back from the kitchen, carrying a casserole, he was snoring softly. She looked at him for a moment and wondered whether or not she should wake him. He looked much too comfortable, and she decided against it. Quietly she sat down at the table and dished up supper for one.

Feeling that she had exhausted the touchy problem of Charlie where Mike was concerned, Laura called round the following day to bend Helen's ear with the facts of the case.

'It's not that I mind Mike working late,' she explained. 'He's done that before. What I mind is him working late because he simply won't face up to the facts about Charlie.' She was well into her stride now and she didn't notice that her sister seemed strangely abstracted. 'And so far as company goes in the evenings,' she continued, 'well, that's a complete write-off. He just comes in, says "hello", sits down, and drops off.'

Helen's face suddenly crumpled and she burst into tears. 'I wish Phil would!' she sobbed.

Laura looked alarmed. She immediately went over to her sister and took her in her arms. 'What's the matter?'

'Oh, nothing. Everything,' Helen said hopelessly.

'But how can it be? You're having a baby.'

Helen pushed her sister away abruptly. 'That's the silliest thing I've ever heard in my life! Why should being pregnant make everything perfect?'

Unusually for her, Laura was at a loss for words. 'Well . . .' she began feebly, and then paused.

'Yes, "Well". It's not all it's cracked up to be – and I've got another seven months of it in store.' Just thinking about this was enough to set Helen off again and she started to sob uncontrollably.

Laura gave her a hankie and put an arm around her shoulders. 'You're just depressed. Think of the end result.'

'If I think of the end result, I get really depressed.'

'You were every so happy last week.'

'Oh yes. I'd just stopped being sick every morning last week.'

'Well, that's something, isn't it?'

'No, it's not something. Now I'm just off it altogether.' It was obvious that Helen had no intention of being consoled.

'Off it? Off what?' Laura asked.

Helen sighed heavily and gave her sister a look.

'Oh. That "it".'

'Yes.'

'Off it?'

'Right off.'

'It's not really that important, is it?'

'It is to me,' Helen wailed. 'I like it! Well, I used to – when I was a proper unpregnant woman. I liked it. Not now, though. Oh – babies!'

Laura was beginning to run out of soothing things to say and, as she didn't particularly consider herself to be an expert on sexual matters, she couldn't really comment usefully on this aspect of the problem either.

They heard someone at the front door and Phil called out, 'Hello, love! I'm home!'

'Stop him, Laura. I'm a mess.' Helen dashed over to the sink and started to splash cold water over her tear-stained face.

Laura no longer felt useless. This was a situation she thought she could handle. Purposefully she strode towards the living-room. 'I'll stop him all right,' she said grimly.

Blissfully unaware of the emotional scene that had been going on in the kitchen, Phil was about to go through to greet his wife when Laura suddenly popped up like a Demon Queen out of a stage trap. She stood in the doorway and barred him from going into the kitchen.

'Oh, hello, Laura. Where's Helen?'

'In there,' she said, her eyes gleaming with the light of battle. Phil went to go in but she pushed him back into the living-room. 'Just a minute. I've got something to say to you.'

'All right. Shoot.'

'Helen is my sister!' Laura announced seriously.

'Is she?' Phil said, flinging his arms up in the air in mock surprise.

'Don't be funny. You know what I'm talking about. Is it really that important?'

'Is what?'

'Sex.'

'Well . . .' That was a tough one.

'It isn't the only thing in the world, you know. I mean, is it such a sacrifice to go without it for a time?'

'No.'

'You've got the bare-faced effrontery to stand there and say "No"?' she said, her voice raised in anger.

'I'll sit down and say it if you like. You've got hold of the wrong end of the stick. It's a habit of yours.' Phil was beginning to tire of this ridiculous cross-examination.

'Then why should my sister be so upset?'

Phil opened his mouth to say something, but that was as far as he got.

'I'll tell you,' Laura said grimly. 'You! What right have you got to make her feel guilty? Good Lord, it's not a whim on her part. It's something to do with pregnancy – something that you obviously don't understand.'

Now what Laura didn't know was that Phil was holding the trump card here. Phil was now the world's expert on pregnancy and its biological, physical and mental effects.

'Yes, I do. Sexual desire – or libido, if you like – is often reduced in pregnancy, especially during the first fourteen weeks,' he said, word-perfect.

The Demon Queen was routed and took a step backwards in surprise. 'Yes – something like that,' she mumbled. 'That's roughly it.'

'In other words, I know what I'm talking about and you don't.'

'You're shifting your ground,' Laura accused.

'I'm not. You're up the paddle without a creek.'

'Creek without a paddle,' she corrected smugly.

Helen, who had heard the raised voices, appeared weepily from the kitchen. 'What are you doing?' she asked in amazement.

'I'm sorry, Helen, but someone has to make this sex maniac understand what you're feeling.'

'But he does. He's being lovely about it. That's why I feel so rotten.'

Helen started to sniffle again. Phil went to her and took her tenderly in his arms. It was a touching scene, and Laura stood around feeling very small indeed.

'If you pretended, very hard, that I hadn't been here today, I would appreciate it,' she said submissively, and she quietly slunk out of the front door. If she'd had a tail it would have been well and truly between her legs.

At Mike's office, the following day, Laura found herself back on duty behind the complaints desk. Her first call was from her friend Mr Miller who wanted to know why Mike wasn't where he should be – in his garden, laying a lawn.

'Look, Mr Miller,' Laura said smoothly. 'I think that you and I have established an understanding now whereby you know that I don't lie to you – I don't flannel. . . I tell you the exact truth . . . Quite. So, I'm happy to tell you that Mr Selway left about five minutes ago and is on his way to see you now . . . Yes. Goodbye.'

She hung up and turned round in time to see Mike walking through the office door. 'I'm starving,' he said as he sat down at his desk and eagerly produced his lunch-box.

'What are you doing?' Laura demanded.

'Well, I thought I'd be totally self-indulgent and take ten whole minutes off for lunch.'

'But you can't. Look, I've got Mr Miller to a point where I tell him the truth and he believes me – and I said you left five minutes ago.'

'You always tell the truth?'

Laura shrugged vaguely as though to imply 'nearly always'.

Mike picked up his lunch-box, stuffed his sandwiches back inside and said, 'I'll eat on the way.' As he got to the door he remembered something. 'Oh, I'll be late again tonight. Charlie was discharged from hospital this morning. I thought I'd pop round and see him.' He waited for the inevitable reaction and was surprised when none came. He stared at Laura, waiting for her to speak.

'What?' she asked, looking back at him.

'I thought you'd have something to say,' he said warily.

'No.'

'Nothing at all?'

'No. Well, don't look so suspicious. I am capable of not rushing in with an opinion.'

'When was this?' Mike asked, feeling he must have missed the occasion.

'One more remark like that and I shall ring Mr Miller and tell him you left two hours ago,' she threatened. 'Give my love to Charlie,' she said, as Mike was about to leave.

Somewhat unexpectedly, Mike walked over, leant over the desk and planted a kiss on her cheek.

Laura was curled up in an armchair, deeply engrossed in a book on pregnancy which she had cadged from Phil. He had parted with it somewhat reluctantly but, as Helen pointed out, he knew it all off by heart now anyway.

'How was Charlie?' she asked as Mike arrived home late that evening.

'Fine. He's fine,' Mike said, with a great deal more conviction than he felt. He went over to the drinks table. 'Do you want a drink?' he asked as he poured one for himself.

'No thanks. How fine is fine?'

'Well, very much his old self really. He didn't have a good word to say about the hospital, the doctors, the nurses, the food. He even grumbled because some kind soul had his cap cleaned.'

Laura got straight to it. 'When is he coming back to work?'

'It's hard to believe you're the same girl who cried her eyes out when we went to see *Bambi*.'

Laura got up and went to sit next to Mike on the sofa. 'It's because I'm worried about you, Mike,' she said. 'You're asleep on your feet half the time these days.'

'I know.'

'You cried as well,' she accused, referring back to *Bambi*.

'I had something in my eye.'

'Liar.'

'I did drop a few hints to Charlie – you know, about keeping his job open.'

'What did he say?'

'He said he'd call a strike if I didn't.'

'He's not even in a union.'

'He didn't look that grand,' Mike confessed. 'He seemed smaller.'

'He wasn't very big to start with.'

'And he looked old. I've never thought of Charlie as old. I know he is, but I've always thought of him as Charlie.'

'Peter Pan in a flat cap.'

'He sent his love, by the way. "Love to Bossy Boots," he said.'

Laura smiled. 'Old devil. What all this boils down to is that he still reckons he'll be back to work.'

'Except I'm not sure he will.'

'But you didn't . . .?'

'How could I?'

'No. How could you?'

'It will sort itself out.'

'Oh yes.'

'Sooner or later.'

'. . . or later.'

Mike was beginning to feel depressed. He didn't want to talk about Charlie any more and so he picked up a newspaper and pretended to read it. Laura took the hint and went back to her armchair. She looked across at Mike but he didn't look up, so she picked up her book on pregnancy and started reading where she'd left off. After a few peaceful minutes had passed, Mike glanced idly over the top of his paper to see whether or not Laura was sulking. His eyes widened considerably as he saw the title of the book Laura was reading. He disappeared back behind his newspaper and tried to collect his thoughts. Happily unaware of the emotional turmoil going on behind the sports page, Laura carried on reading.

It didn't take Helen long to get out of the doldrums, and she quickly became her usual sunny self again. She and Phil were enjoying a quiet breakfast together when they caught sight of Mike hovering outside the kitchen window. They exchanged looks of resignation, and Phil got up to let him in. Helen and Phil knew that these early-morning visits boded no good as far as the Continuing Story of Mike and Laura was concerned. Neither one of them said anything, but waited for Mike to speak. They didn't have to wait for very long. As soon as he had sat down at the table Mike said, 'Has Laura told you anything that she might not have told me?'

'Mike,' Phil said, 'we're very fond of you, we really are, but you simply must stop this habit of calling in on your way to work – early – and asking bizarre questions.'

Mike chose to ignore this heartfelt plea and merely said, 'Well?'

'I suppose she must have done,' Helen said.

'What?'

'I don't know – things. I expect you've told Phil things that you wouldn't tell Laura.'

Phil chuckled out loud at this. It was a rather naughty chuckle.

Mike seemed to remember something and he and Phil exchanged grins. 'Yes, well that was . . . I'm talking about serious things.'

Helen thought for a while. 'When she was ten she told me she wanted to be a missionary.'

'Lately. I mean lately.'

'Now look, Mike. I'm not disclosing any of Laura's confidences – assuming there are any – without you being more specific.'

'Well, it's a bit personal.'

'Would you like to write it down so that you don't have to say it aloud?' Phil asked.

Taking a deep breath, Mike said, 'Is she pregnant?'

This was the last thing Phil and Helen were expecting and for several moments they sat there looking at him open-mouthed.

'I don't know,' Helen said.

'Well, I certainly don't,' Phil said.

'Neither do I,' Mike said.

'Laura would know,' Phil suggested.

'Of course she would,' Mike said.

'Then be devious,' Phil advised. 'Ask her.'

Mike looked worried. 'She'd tell me if she was, wouldn't she?'

'What makes you think she might be?' Helen asked.

'Well, she was reading a book.'

'No, that's not how it happens,' Phil joked, unable to resist the feed line.

'Phil!' Helen chided, then turned to Mike. 'What sort of book?'

'About pregnancy.'

'Oh, that book,' Phil said. 'That's mine. I lent it to her.'

'Why?'

'Because we had a bit of a . . . discussion . . . the other day . . .'

'About me,' Helen said.

'And Laura discovered that women don't automatically know everything about pregnancy.'

'*Some* women,' Helen admonished.

'*Some* women. So I lent her the book.'

'That must be it, then,' Mike said, with evident relief.

'Yes.'

'Unless . . .' Helen said slowly, beginning to wonder if there was another, more interesting motive.

Mike began to look worried again. 'Yes,' he said. 'Anyway, thanks. I'd better get off to work.'

'Now what was that about?' Phil asked, after he'd left.

'What?'

'That "Unless . . ." '

'Well, it's Mike. He's living with her and, if he hasn't got the gumption to ask her himself, he deserves to sweat a little.'

'Perhaps she doesn't want the subject raised at all . . . She wouldn't, would she?'

Helen smiled secretively. 'It has been known.'

'Without telling him?'

'That has been known as well.'

Laura joined Mike for a picnic lunch at the office at midday. She was reading The Book again and not particularly enjoying the part she was looking at. Mike kept casting worried glances in her direction. You were supposed to be able to tell if a woman was pregnant by the look in her eyes, but he wasn't quite sure exactly *what* the look looked like.

'You know, I'm not sure that pregnancy is all it's cracked up to be,' Laura said, putting her book down.

'No?' Mike said, trying to sound casual.

'Perhaps I'm just not naturally maternal.'

'Probably not,' he assured her.

'Helen is. She wanted this baby so badly, but even she . . . I mean, if Helen can't cope with it all the time, what chance do I stand?'

Mike, who was desperately looking for clues as to Laura's current condition, latched on to the tense she had used. 'Do?'

'Well . . . would.'

Mike double-checked. 'Would?' he repeated.

'You seem very concerned about tenses.'

'Aren't *you*?'

'Why should I be?'

'Because there is a considerable difference between "do" and "would" – an important difference. So is it "do" or "would"?'

'Is what?' Laura said, trying to follow the reasoning behind all this and failing to see what Mike was getting at.

'Are you pregnant?'

'Of course I'm not pregnant,' she laughed. Then

she looked down at the book. The penny dropped. 'Oh, this?' she said.

'Yes. It's not exactly what you'd call light reading, is it?'

'If I were reading a book on mountaineering, you wouldn't assume that I was about to go tearing up the nearest Alp, would you?'

'Why were you reading it, then?' he persisted.

'For Helen. I want to be as supportive as I can, but I've discovered that I don't really know what to be supportive about. Anyway, I wouldn't spring a baby on you, Mike. We'd have to decide. We'd have to talk about it. We'd have to want one.'

Mike had already made his decision. 'Well, we don't, do we?' he said.

'No, I don't think so,' Laura said.

Mike relaxed immediately and went back to his lunch feeling a much happier and freer man. If he'd caught sight of Laura's face just a few seconds later, he might not have felt so sanguine. She was just beginning to give the question of motherhood some serious thought. Now the subject was out in the open, she felt it was something she'd like to discuss in more depth. She looked at her book with a slightly more subjective interest than formerly, and was just about to say something to Mike when there was a tap at the door and a middle-aged, harrassed-looking woman wearing a felt hat limped into the office.

'Mr Selway, is it?' the woman asked.

Mike stood up. 'Yes. May I help you?'

'I'm Jessie Harris – Charlie's sister.'

'Is he all right?' Mike asked, fearing the worst.

'Oh, he's all right, all right. Sitting there, giving his orders.' She turned and looked Laura up and down. 'I dare say you'd be . . .'

'Bossy Boots,' Laura affirmed.

'Yes,' Jessie said, without a trace of a smile. 'Do you mind if I sit down? My leg's giving me gyp.'

'Yes, of course,' Mike said, pulling out a chair for the visitor.

She sat down with melodramatic relief and stretched one of her legs out in front of her. 'How I ever got it up here from Romford, I'll never know. Any tea in the pot?' she asked, looking and sounding for a split second just like Charlie.

'I'll get you some,' Laura offered.

'Funny,' Jessie said, watching Laura closely, 'I had you down as a big woman.'

'Sorry,' Laura apologized. 'So how is Charlie?'

'Like I said. Sitting there like Lord Muck giving his orders. Do this. Do that. Run here. Run there. I haven't been able to run anywhere since the Coronation.'

Laura handed her a cup of tea.

'Ta very much.' She looked around the office with a critical eye. 'Mmmmm. Charlie said it wasn't Buckingham Palace.'

'Mrs Harris, did Charlie ask you to come?' Mike said, feeling that maybe there was an important message he should know about.

'Told. Told me,' she grumbled.

'What about?'

'About keeping his job open.'

'Oh. Well, I am doing that,' Mike reassured her. He was expecting some small sign of gratitude; he certainly wasn't prepared for the response he got.

'Then you must be dafter than you look,' Jessie said with considerable satisfaction. 'You saw him the other night.'

'I thought he looked pretty chipper.'

'Chipper?' she sniffed.

'Well . . . considering.'

'There'll always be a place for Charlie here, he knows that,' Laura said.

'You're as daft as he is,' Jessie said bluntly. 'Charlie won't be coming back.'

Laura was beginning to take a dislike to this woman. 'I'd have thought that was for Charlie to say,' she said.

'Right!' Mike agreed.

'He has,' Jessie announced. 'Only – typical Charlie – he gets somebody else to do his dirty work for him.'

'But when I talked to him the other night – '

'Hot air. Well, not just hot air. He didn't want to let you down.'

'Good old Charlie,' Mike said, smiling softly.

'What will he do?' Laura asked, beginning to feel rather concerned about him.

'He's coming to live with me in the bungalow at Romford. He'll be all right. We row all the time, but we've always got on, me and Charlie. Of course, if he thinks it's going to be a permanent convalescence, he's got another think coming.'

'I wish he'd have come himself,' Mike said sadly.

'I think he would have – only he likes you. He asked me to give you this.' She handed Mike a rather grubby envelope. Mike swallowed hard. He was deeply touched that old Charlie had remembered him. 'I should get him something,' he said.

'You already did,' Jessie said. 'I can't think of many who'd have put up with him as long as you did. Well, I'd best be off.' It took her several laborious moments to struggle to her feet.

'Can we get you a cab, or something?' Laura asked.

'No, thanks. If Charlie's coming to live, I've got to get used to dashing around.' Jessie didn't look as if she could dash anywhere.

'Tell him . . . tell him . . .' Mike couldn't really put

his true feelings into words. 'Give him my best,' he said finally.

'And mine,' Laura added.

'Of course I will. Good-bye, then.'

'Good-bye.'

Jessie made her way painfully out of the door. Mike tore open the envelope and read Charlie's message. Laura looked at his face. Whatever was in the note had obviously touched Mike deeply.

'Old skiver,' he said, smiling fondly.

Jessie limped back in through the door again. 'Oh, I nearly forgot,' she said. 'He said the teapot was his.' She picked it up, still warm from the tea, and walked out with it.

Mike was relaxing on the sofa after yet another exhausting day's work when Laura gave him the good news – the long hours were beginning to pay off at last and now they were only two weeks behind.

'I wonder what the new bloke will be like,' Mike considered.

'Have you got one?'

'No. I just wonder what he'll be like.'

'How about a compulsive worker?'

'That would do,' Mike yawned.

'You look whacked. Why don't you go to bed?'

'No. I've been so busy, I don't seem to have seen anything of you lately, and all we've had time to talk about is work.'

'All right. Let's chat.'

'Charlie will be all right with his sister, won't he?' Mike said, beginning to look concerned.

After several weeks of living through the Good Old Charlie crisis, this was the last thing Laura wanted to discuss. 'Mike!' she warned.

'Sorry.'

'I phoned Helen this afternoon,' Laura said.

'How is she?'

'Much better.'

'I didn't know she'd been ill.'

'Not exactly ill – a bit peculiar.'

'Helen? Did Phil know about this?'

'Oh yes, he knew. It worried me for a bit, seeing Helen off-balance ... well, it borders on the unnerving.'

'Yes,' Mike agreed. 'Of course, hormonal changes during pregnancy do have some side-effects.'

'How did you know that?' Laura asked in amazement.

'I read it in that book of Phil's.'

'Oh, that book,' she grimaced.

'Puts you right off, doesn't it?'

'Yes,' she said slowly.

'Those diagrams are the worst.' Mike started to yawn again. He was very near to falling asleep.

Laura looked pensive. 'Mind you,' she said, 'when you think of the end result ... when you think of Helen and Phil with a little Philette or Helenette ...' She smiled warmly at this. 'I'm probably just being silly but, round about my age, perhaps you start to think it will soon be too late, and then do you regret it? I don't know. Quite honestly, Mike, it's been on my mind a lot lately and ... well, it would help if we talked about it.' She deliberately didn't look at him as she said this. Taking his silence for interest, she went on. 'I'm not sure Mike – I'm really not – but I'm beginning to think that I'd like to have a baby.'

Having got this off her chest at last, she turned round quickly to gauge Mike's immediate reaction. He was sound asleep.

'We could always settle for a budgerigar,' she said very loudly.

162

Mike was startled awake. 'Um? What?' he mumbled.

Laura looked at his dazed face. 'Nothing,' she said.

8

Mike was wearing his best suit and sitting stiffly to attention. Suits always seemed to have this formal effect upon him, but today there was an additional stress factor: he was due to interview several applicants for Charlie's old job.

He looked anxiously at an empty chair facing his desk, then carefully moved an angle-poise lamp to his left. Phil, who was there as adviser, watched this performance with some amusement. Strangely enough, Laura, who was sitting at her desk reading a book, seemed totally uninterested in the whole business and was offering no advice whatsoever.

'What do you think, Phil?' Mike asked. 'There? Or there?' And he moved the lamp again.

'I can't see your face at all now,' Phil said.

'Oh, no.' Mike moved the lamp to his right. 'There, then? So that the light shines on the interviewee. What about that?'

'Mike, you're interviewing applicants for a job, not questioning suspects.'

'I've run out of places to put it,' Mike said. By now he seemed to consider the lamp to be a vital part of the proceedings.

Laura, who was just beginning to be irritated by this constant rearrangement of the office furniture, picked up the lamp and dumped it down in the middle of her own desk.

'Yes,' Mike said. 'Better idea.' After all, it was one less thing to worry about. Knowing him, he'd probably hit his head on it at a vital moment. 'Now let me run through it again, Phil. Not too remote – not too friendly – and let them do most of the talking.'

'And write things down.'

'What things?'

'Anything – a shopping list, if you like. But, so long as you write something down from time to time, you keep them off-balance.'

'Right,' Mike said. He'd try it, but he didn't honestly believe he had the cold Machiavellian cunning essential to this approach. 'Thanks for the coaching. I've never actually done this before.'

'What about Charlie? You must have interviewed him when he came for the job?'

'Not really, no,' Mike said. 'He just walked in, said, "I'm Charlie. Any tea in the pot?", and we sort of went on from there.'

'Pretty incisive interviewing.'

'Still, it worked out all right. I mean, we always had a pot of tea on the go after that.'

'You want someone who's prepared to work as hard as you, not someone who wants a cup of tea every five minutes,' Phil warned.

'You're quite right,' Mike agreed. He looked around nervously.

'Anyone fancy a cup of tea?'

'No thanks. I've got to go home and start redecorating the spare room,' Phil said.

Laura immediately looked up at this and said, 'Nursery.'

'All right – nursery.'

'Anyway, thanks for the advice, Phil,' Mike said.

'For what it's worth. I've never interviewed blokes. I've only ever interviewed secretaries.'

'That must be much nicer,' Mike said.

'Scenically,' Phil grinned.

'That's what I mean.'

Laura thought that this conversation was getting decidedly silly. 'Are you doing the nursery in blue or pink?' she demanded.

'Apricot,' Phil said.

'Mmmmmm.' Laura considered this carefully.

Phil prepared to leave. 'Right,' he said, 'I'm off to get paint all up my arms. Good luck, Mike – and don't give somebody the job just because they've got nice legs.'

Laura got to her feet. 'Hope you get somebody good, Mike,' she said.

'Aren't you staying?' Mike asked.

'No. I'd just be in the way. I'd interfere.'

'I'm used to that,' Mike said, fully expecting her to rise to the bait. Surprisingly, she didn't.

'No, it's your business,' she said quietly. 'You know what you're looking for.'

Mike stared at her and wondered if she were sickening for something. She did look a bit pale.

'Give you a lift, Laura?' Phil offered. 'Drop you off somewhere?'

'Well, actually, I thought I'd come back with you – have a natter with Helen,' she said.

This suggestion didn't exactly get an enthusiastic response from Phil. It seemed to him that Laura had been spending far too much time in their house lately, and there were times when her interference got on his nerves.

'It's been quite a time,' she said lightly, not daring to look him in the face as she said this.

'Yes,' Phil said ironically. 'It must be all of yesterday.'

'You don't mind, do you?' she pleaded.

'No,' he said, feeling a bit mean. 'I only warn you, you'll end up with a paintbrush in your hand.'

Mike was beginning to get the unmistakable symptoms of stage fright. This was one of those occasions when he'd like to have Laura around to give him some moral support. 'I mean, *you'll* have to work with the bloke as well.'

'Only part-time,' she said dismissively. 'No, it's much more important that you find somebody you can get on with. After all, I might not be here for ever.'

She *was* sickening for something and hadn't told him. An incurable disease, perhaps. 'What do you mean?'

'Nothing. I just might not be able to come and help out here for ever. See you later,' she said, and walked through the door.

Phil followed her, after giving Mike a questioning look. Mike shrugged vaguely. Who could fathom Laura when she was in a mood like this? She was up to something, though, of that he was sure. After they'd both left, he considered the problem of the angle-poise lamp again.

As soon as she got inside Phil and Helen's house, Laura bustled around happily, trying to make herself as useful as possible. She made Helen sit down and put her feet up while she prepared some tea. Phil wisely decided to disappear upstairs and carry on with the painting.

Laura carried the tea-tray into the living-room. 'I brought you some biscuits as well – custard creams.'

'Ughhhhh!' Helen pulled a face.

'They're your favourites.'

'Not any more.'

'Oh.' Laura looked disappointed. 'These things you go off? Do you ever go back on them?'

Helen smiled – a warm, secret smile. 'Some of them.'

'Oh, I'm glad.'

167

'Phil's rather pleased as well,' Helen said, looking smug.

Laura suddenly noticed that Helen was sitting with her legs crossed. 'You're not supposed to sit like that,' she said bossily. 'Come on.' And she lifted her sister's legs up on to the sofa.

'According to popular fiction, husbands are supposed to fuss, not sisters.'

'What does he know that I don't?'

'It's temperament, isn't it? You know Phil – he tends to simply take things in his stride.' There was an anguished shout from upstairs that belied this remark. 'Except when he's painting,' Helen qualified.

'He's perfectly formed,' Laura said.

Helen looked askance at this unexpected compliment. 'Phil?'

'Not Phil. The baby. After thirteen weeks the baby is perfectly formed.' She sighed. 'It's wonderful, isn't it?'

'If you go on like this, you're going to get sympathetic labour pains.'

'They must be wonderful too, in their own way,' Laura said, her eyes shining with the sheer romance of it all.

'Oh, terrific! I'm really looking forward to them.'

'When you've got a child – a tiny, perfect child inside you, do you feel fulfilled?'

The more romantic and high-flown Laura became, the more realistic and down-to-earth Helen felt. 'Full,' she said. Laura looked distinctly disappointed. 'Oh, I don't know – different.'

'Wonderful?' Laura suggested.

'Not wonderful – different.'

'Will you have more?'

'Give me a chance. I haven't had this one yet.'

'I bet you will. I think that's wonderful.' That word again.

'Laura, I don't know whether you're aware of it, but you are gushing.'

'I am not,' Laura said, indignantly.

'You are. Wonderful this – wonderful that. You even think that having to get up to go to the loo in the middle of the night is wonderful.'

'Well, it is.'

'You try it!'

'I might.'

'What?'

'Well . . . I might,' Laura said, realizing that she quite liked the idea.

'You mean that you and Mike have decided . . .'

'No – I haven't actually raised the subject with Mike yet.'

'Don't you think you'd better?'

'Yes.' She thought carefully about this aspect. She'd have to get him in the right mood, of course, before she broached the subject. 'I'll do chips tonight. He likes chips.'

'Laura, I'm not being rotten, but this isn't just because I . . . I mean, you're not simply feeling a bit broody are you?'

'I don't know,' she admitted. 'I might be. I did think about babies. Then I didn't – I didn't for a long time. But the years go by and my only claim to youth is being younger than Jane Fonda and that's not fair – I mean look at her . . . well, I haven't got all that much time left, have I?'

Helen looked worried. She was convinced that this was not at all the right reason for getting pregnant. She started to say something but just then Phil came downstairs, carrying two paintbrushes.

'What happened to equal rights?' he said.

Helen got up quickly. 'Sorry,' she apologized. 'We've been talking.'

Laura was instantly on the defensive. 'You can't

paint,' she said to Helen. 'You can't stand the smell of paint.'

'I do now. I like it.'

'All right, Auntie?' Phil said, grinning annoyingly.

'For your information,' Laura said, 'there may be another auntie in this room.'

It took Phil a little while to work this one out. 'You mean, you and Mike . . . ?'

'Maybe.'

'You and Mike?'

'Yes.'

Phil shook with laughter.

Mike had finally decided to reinstate the angle-poise lamp on his desk – it gave him an air of authority he felt that he somehow lacked. He checked for the umpteenth time that he had a pencil and pad to hand and then cleared his throat a couple of times. Just then, the door opened and a young man in his early twenties, casually dressed in jeans and a bomber jacket and carrying a hold-all, popped his head round the door.

'Mr Selway,' he said in a lively Cockney accent, 'I'm Terry Bullivant. The Job Centre sent me.'

'Oh yes. Have a seat.' Mike cleared his throat again and moved the lamp half a centimetre to the left.

Terry breezed in, sat down and put his hold-all on the floor. He was totally at ease and looked about him, taking his time.

As soon as he felt he had Terry's attention, Mike spoke. 'Now then . . .' He leaned forward and knocked his head sharply on the lamp. He moved it back to Laura's desk. 'Now then,' he repeated.

'I can only stay ten minutes,' Terry said.

Mike began to feel flustered. This wasn't how it was supposed to be. The applicant should be more deferential, possibly even slightly cowed. Remembering Phil's advice about gaining the psychological advantage, Mike picked up his pencil and tried to look dominant. 'Well, that's very magnaminous of you,' he said sarcastically.

'No, that's not meant against you,' Terry confided. 'Only I've got to feed the baby at twelve.' Mike wasn't expecting this at all – Phil had said nothing about interviewees feeding babies.

'Baby?' Mike said, putting down his pencil.

'Yes, she's out there.' Terry got up, crossed to the window and pointed proudly.

Mike stood up and looked over his shoulder. There was indeed a baby in a pink bonnet sitting in a pram outside.

'Hello, Alana,' Terry called, waving through the window. 'All right?' He turned to Mike. 'Wave,' he encouraged. 'She likes being waved at.'

Mike found himself doing a self-conscious little wave.

'Look, Mr Bullivant,' he said, trying to get back to the business in hand.

'Terry.'

'Terry. This is rather unusual, isn't it?'

'What?'

'Well . . .' Mike gestured vaguely towards the window.

'Oh, Alana, you mean? Well, I had to bring her because Cheryl is at work – she's on the till.'

'I see,' Mike said, although he couldn't quite follow the reasoning behind this. 'Shall we . . .?' He waved towards the seat and was relieved when Terry sat down again and he could get behind the desk once more. 'But if your wife . . .'

'Cheryl,' Terry reminded him.

'Cheryl. If she works and you're after the job here, who would look after the baby?'

'Alana.'

'Alana. Yes. Would Cheryl give up her job?'

'Oh, no. She earns more than you're offering here. That's fair, mind, because she has got two CSEs,' Terry announced proudly.

'Well, who will look after Alana?'

'Oh, no sweat. My mum. Only she couldn't today because she had to go to the solicitor's about Edie's shoulder.'

'I see.' Mike was still confused but decided that it was probably best not to pursue the matter any further. 'Right, then.' He picked up his pencil. 'Have you been out of work long?'

'Eleven months – the day after we conceived of Alana. That's a twist, isn't it?' Terry said, giving a wry smile but not seeming to hold any grudge against fate.

Mike didn't want to get back on to the subject of babies again so carefully didn't comment on this. 'Yes. And what sort of job had you done before that?'

'Oh, yards of them.'

'Pardon?'

'All sorts.'

'What was the last one?' Mike asked, determined to pin Terry down so he could write something on his pad.

'I done a movie.'

'Are you an actor?'

'No. You never had to act. It was a blue movie.'

Mike considered making a note of this, but then decided against it. It didn't seem particularly relevant. 'What was that like?' he asked curiously.

'Cold,' Terry said. He picked up his bag and suddenly produced a baby's bottle with milk in it. 'Would you mind if I warmed this up?'

'No,' Mike said, feeling he couldn't very well refuse.

'I've got all the gear,' Terry said cheerfully, and

went over to switch the kettle on. He delved down into his bag again and produced a small saucepan.

'About the job,' Mike said, desperately.

'Oh, sure. Yes. Carry on.'

'How much do you know about it?'

'Well, it's gardening, isn't it?' Terry said.

'Landscape gardening,' Mike said seriously.

'What's the difference?'

'Well, quite a lot. There's design.'

'Sorry. Couldn't help you there,' Terry admitted disarmingly.

'No, I do that. A certain amount of construction, paths, rockeries, patios.'

'Posh gardening?' Terry said, beginning to get the idea.

'In a way – sometimes,' Mike agreed doubtfully.

'Now you could be talking – about construction, I mean – because I was in the building trade once.'

Now they were getting somewhere. Mike prepared to write down the relevant facts. 'Ah! How long for?'

'About six weeks.'

Mike sighed and put down his pencil. Terry meanwhile busied himself sterilizing the baby's bottle in his saucepan.

'What about gardening *per se*?' Mike said, bravely battling on against all the odds.

Terry frowned. 'Per who?'

'As such,' Mike translated.

'Well, I was in the Parks one summer.'

'Excellent.' He wrote this down.

'That was only picking up paper, though . . .'

'Oh.' He scratched it out again.

Terry didn't seem at all apologetic or worried about his apparent lack of qualifications for the job. He smiled and said brightly, 'Still, it's mostly common sense, isn't it? I mean, you dig holes, stick the plants in and they grow.'

'I wish it were that simple. You see, if I stick plants in holes for a customer and those plants don't grow, the customer tends to blame me.'

'What about dogs?'

'Dogs?'

'Yes. What if the customer has a dog and the dog tiddles on the plants. That's not your fault, is it? You're a gardener, not a dog handler.'

'Landscape gardener,' Mike corrected.

'Sorry, yes.' He took the bottle of milk from the saucepan and expertly squeezed a small amount of milk on the back of his hand. 'You'll be seeing other people?'

'Five or six.'

The baby began to cry and Terry looked up. 'There she goes,' he said, smiling proudly. 'On the dot. Is it all right if I feed her outside? Then I'll come back for my saucepan and shoot off.'

'There's nowhere for you to sit down out there. You'd better bring her in.' In for a penny, Mike thought. Anyway, he'd long since lost control of the interview. He had nothing to lose now.

'Ta,' Terry said, and went out. Mike looked down at his pad – there was nothing there worth keeping. Terry reappeared carrying little Alana. He took up the bottle, sat down and started to feed her expertly. 'She won't be long,' he said as Mike looked on. 'She's a right little guzzler, aren't you Alana, eh?' Alana gurgled happily.

Mike watched and found himself smiling as he viewed the cosy domestic scene between father and child.

That evening, as he and Laura got ready to go to bed, Mike told her all about Terry, Alana, Edie's shoulder and Cheryl. Laura showed a great deal of interest in the baby and seemed to take an immediate liking to Terry, sight unseen, mainly because he was a young father.

'But you didn't give him the job?' she asked anxiously.

'I've got three more blokes coming tomorrow,' Mike pointed out. 'I can't not see them.'

'But he came top of today's three.' She was determined now that Terry should be given the job.

'Yes. I liked him.' Mike had been giving the situation a great deal of thought. 'I just wish I was sure he didn't bring that baby deliberately. If I see him again, I've got a suspicion that he might turn up with his old grannie – in a wheelchair.'

'What was the baby like?' Laura asked eagerly.

'All right – in a belchy sort of way.'

Mike climbed into bed and picked up his book. Laura picked up her book, but clearly her mind wasn't on it. She took a sideways look at Mike, then taking a deep breath she said:

'Mike?'

'Um?'

'I think I'd like to have a baby.'

Mike stared hard at his book. He didn't look up and hoped desperately that, if he pretended he hadn't heard, the question might go away. It didn't.

'Did you hear what I said?'

'Yes.'

'Well, say something, then.'

'You're too old.'

'I am not,' she said indignantly.

He looked doubtful. 'Are you sure?'

'Of course I'm sure. Women these days . . .' She reconsidered. 'Oldish,' she admitted. 'But that's the thing, you see. If I don't fairly soon, then I would be too old.'

'There you are, then.' He said this matter-of-factly,

in the tone of voice that indicated the discussion was at an end, but Laura would not accept defeat.

'There I am, then, what?' she said, trying to draw him out.

'What?' he said, although he'd heard perfectly well.

'What point are you making?'

'It's no reason, is it?' He put his book down. 'It's a bit like swilling down the pint you don't really want because you know the barman's going to call "Time".'

'What a charming analogy!'

'You know what I mean.'

'Yes, I do, and you're wrong. There's more to it than that.'

'You never mentioned babies,' he said accusingly.

'When?'

'When we got together.'

'I don't remember you issuing a typed list of preconditions for our relationship.'

'You don't, do you?'

'No, you just cross your fingers and hope that things are going to be all right.'

'Well, they are, aren't they?'

'Yes,' she said grudgingly.

'So why go mucking about with them?'

'I'm not mucking about with anything.'

'I thought we were all right as we were,' Mike said.

'We are.'

'Well, then?'

'They could be better.'

'By having a baby?'

'Well, don't make it seem so incredible.'

'I can't see us with a baby. Can you honestly see us with a baby? My God, we're a big enough shambles on our own.'

Laura latched on to this immediately. 'So you actually think that our relationship is a shambles,' she said accusingly.

'No,' he sighed wearily.

'That's what you said.'

'I didn't mean it like that. I simply mean that . . . well, we haven't been together that long . . . and it's been a pretty bumpy ride and I don't think you solve anything by starting to throw babies into the arena.'

'I am not throwing babies into the arena! I'm just saying that I think I'd like one.'

'There you go again – "think". You can't return a baby to the shop, you know. You can't have a baby on approval.'

The sheer condescension of this little homily made Laura see red. 'I love you when you're constructive,' she said sarcastically.

'If you want the truth, I think you're just going broody.'

'I am not a hen,' she said huffily. Something occurred to her. 'Helen said that.'

He had her there. 'Aha!' he said waving his finger at her.

'Aha, what?'

At last he'd got to the root of the problem. 'Well, that's it, isn't it? Helen's having a baby, so you want a baby. It's like a sister wanting her sister's toys.'

'I never wanted her toys. I never wanted a single one of her toys. She was the one who always wanted *my* toys, and she got them. "Don't be selfish, Laura. Share your toys with Helen. She's only a baby!" '

This recollection of her childhood, combined with the key word 'baby', upset Laura. She felt alone and extremely vulnerable. Mike saw that she was very close to tears and tried a diversionary tactic.

'I never had any proper toys when I was a kid. A cardboard shoebox on a piece of string – that's all I had at the orphanage.'

It was talk like this that usually earned him a quick cuddle, but it wasn't working this time.

'Oh, don't start that orphanage sob-stuff again,' she snapped.

'Then the shoebox got left out in the rain – it disintegrated . . .'

'I don't think you were ever in an orphanage. I think that you are really the son of some nobleman and you're travelling the outside world disguised as a landscape gardener before you go back and take up your inheritance.'

'I did have some soldiers, but their heads kept falling off.'

'I had some soldiers,' she said, suddenly remembering her toy fort.

'I thought little girls played with dolls.' He silently congratulated himself – this was going quite well.

'Not all little girls. No, some little girls don't really develop maternal instincts till much later in life – and you thought you'd got me off the subject, didn't you?'

Angry at being foiled so easily, Mike turned off the lamp. 'We've discussed the subject,' he said firmly, settling down to go to sleep.

'You think so?' Laura said grimly, as he kissed her cheek.

'For tonight, anyway. Sleep tight.'

'Goodnight, Mike,' she said, and switched off her bedside lamp.

There was a tense silence.

'John Paul Jones,' Laura suddenly said, determined not to let sleeping Mikes lie.

'Who?'

'I think it was John Paul Jones,' she repeated.

'What about him?'

'Who said, "I have not yet begun to fight." '

She smiled determinedly to herself under the

covers. Mike was fully awake. He realized he had a problem that wasn't going to go away overnight.

Surprisingly enough, Mike managed to escape to the office the following morning without any further discussions about babies. He sat at his desk and tried to concentrate on a garden plan, but his mind just wasn't on it and he kept going over the conversation he'd had with Laura the previous night.

There was a knock on the door and a middle-aged man, smartly dressed in an expensive three-piece suit, entered the office. Mike looked up.

'Mr Selway? Wilfred Robinson,' the man said in a confident, cultured voice.

Mike immediately jumped to the conclusion that Mr Robinson was a client and got up straight away to shake hands. 'How do you do? Sit down,' he said politely.

'Thank you,' Mr Robinson said, as he sat down and looked around him.

Mike followed his gaze. 'Sorry,' he apologized. 'Bit of a mess. What can I do for you, Mr Robinson?'

Mr Robinson looked rather surprised at this question. 'Quite a lot, I hope.'

'Good, good,' Mike said, and opened his order book. Each waited for the other to speak first. Mr Robinson didn't seem to have anything pertinent to add. 'So. Big job, is it?' Mike prompted.

'That's rather for you to say, isn't it?'

'Well, I can't until I know what it is.'

'But you advertised,' Mr Robinson said, looking a bit confused.

'Yes, I'm in the yellow pages, but that doesn't make me a mind-reader. I can't forecast what jobs people want.' Mike was beginning to have the distinct impression that he could possibly be dealing with some kind of nutcase.

'*The* job, Mr Selway,' Mr Robinson said.

Mike looked bewildered. Mr Robinson was beginning to think that he was dealing with an idiot.

'Did you say "yellow pages"?' Mr Robinson asked, as a faint light began to dawn.

'Yes.'

'I was referring to the advertisement at the Job Centre.'

'You mean you've come about the job?'

'Yes.'

Mike felt extremely foolish. Yet another interview off to a brilliant start. 'I'm sorry, I thought . . .'

'My wife said I should have worn a cardigan,' Mr Robinson said, smiling ruefully.

'No, I . . . you look very nice,' Mike mumbled.

'Thank you.'

'You don't want to work here.'

'Oh, but I do.'

'But what did you use to do?'

'I was a personnel manager for a large manufacturing company but, not to put too fine a point on it, the last thing that the company manufactured was a total collapse.' Mr Robinson smiled ruefully.

'But surely with qualifications like that . . .'

'I don't wish to be rude, Mr Selway, but "surely with qualifications like that" has assumed the proportions of a conversational death-knell. I am fifty years old, and fifty-year-old middle-managers are only minimally less in demand than hula hoops.'

'You've seen the wages I'm offering,' Mike warned.

'Yes.'

'You must have got more than that in luncheon vouchers.'

Mr Robinson did not deny this. 'One must adapt,' he said, with a quiet dignity that impressed Mike.

'Look, be honest, Mr Robinson. How much do you know about gardening?'

'A little. Before we moved, we had a fair-sized garden which we tended ourselves.'

'What do you call fair-sized?' Mike asked in a fairly patronizing voice, knowing that people tended to exaggerate slightly when it came to property.

'Two acres.'

Mike immediately stopped looking patronizing and started looking impressed. 'I know it said "assistant horticulturist" but, when you come down to it, it's really just labouring,' he warned.

'I realize that. I'm very fit.'

'Well . . .' Mike said doubtfully.

Mr Robinson got up. 'I won't take any more of your time, Mr Selway. I'm sure you have other applicants to see. I can, of course, furnish excellent references if required. Thank you for seeing me. Goodbye.'

Mike was tempted to ask Mr Robinson to stay, but he wavered slightly.

As Mr Robinson reached the door, he turned round. His composure was just beginning to slip. 'I want to go home again in the evenings and say, "I've been to work",' he said simply. He closed the door quietly behind him.

Mike sat at his desk and stared at the empty chair. He felt rather shaken and wondered if everybody had the same trouble as he was experiencing with this type of decision-making. The door opened and Terry Bullivant popped his head round.

'Hello, there,' he said cheerfully. 'I just wondered if there was any news.'

Since the baby debate with Mike the previous evening, Laura had been withdrawn and moody, and when Phil and Helen called round for drinks they immediately sensed an 'atmosphere'. Mike started to tell Phil about Terry and Mr Robinson, while Laura sat and stared ahead of her in stony silence.

'He really meant, it, you see,' Mike said. 'I almost ran after him and offered him the job on the spot, but then Terry turned up and I like him as well.'

'He didn't bring the baby with him this time, did he?' Phil asked.

Laura looked up at this. 'Penny in the box, please, Phil. We don't talk about babies here,' she said sarcastically.

By this time everyone was beginning to tire of Laura's 'performance' and by silent mutual consent they chose to ignore it.

'Well, I think you should give Mr Robinson the job,' Helen said to Mike. 'He sounds cuddly.'

'I'm not hiring somebody to cuddle.'

'You cuddle babies,' Laura said, determined not to let the subject drop that easily.

'No, go for the young one,' Phil advised. 'What's that saying about old dogs and new tricks?'

'Well, it's wrong in any case. Older men are steadier – more reliable,' Helen said, speaking up for Mr Robinson.

'What do you know about older men?' Phil asked suspiciously.

'I'm married to one. Anybody over thirty these days is positively geriatric. It must be awful to find you're on the scrap heap at fifty.'

'I thought that,' Mike said.

'Personally. I am firmly resolved to be on the scrap heap at fifty,' Phil said.

'And what do you intend to live on?' Helen asked.

'Charity from all my adoring children,' Phil said, smiling. Then, realizing he had mentioned the forbidden subject, he turned to Laura and apologized.

'I didn't say a word,' she said, still in a sulk.

'I keep tossing up, you see. I wish King Solomon was in the phone book. What do you think, Laura?' Mike said, trying to include her in the conversation.

'I thought you'd become very good at making quick decisions,' she retorted, glaring at him. Mike knew what she was referring to, but he was determined not to be drawn into that old argument – particularly in front of Phil and Helen.

'You said you keep tossing up. Why not spin a coin?' Phil suggested.

Mike shook his head. 'No, it's never any good spinning a coin about big decisions. It always tends to land on a tuft of carpet so that it's not flat – as though it's saying, "I am heads but, if it wasn't for this tuft of carpet, I'd be tails".'

'Mr Robinson must have an awful lot of business experience,' Helen said, speaking up for her favourite.

'Yes, but in personnel,' Mike said. 'If I took him, the only personnel I'd have would be him.'

'He could always take his problems to himself. No, go for young Terry,' Phil advised.

'But he doesn't know the first thing about gardening.'

'I doubt that Mr Robinson knows a great deal about getting his hands dirty,' Phil said.

'Oh, I don't know. I *didn't* imagine it would be this hard. And they're the pick of the bunch – a personnel manager and a blue movie star.'

'But you like them both?' Helen said.

'Yes, I do.'

Laura intervened. 'Well, I should divorce yourself from emotion. Let emotion get into things and it clouds your judgement.'

Mike's temper snapped. 'Oh, do change the record!'

Laura got up and went over to the record player. 'Certainly,' she said. 'What would you like – "Everybody Loves My Baby"?' There was an embarrassed silence at this. Laura realized this was simply not funny. Upset with herself and feeling very close to tears, she ran out of the room.

Mike looked at Phil and Helen. 'I bet you're really glad you came now,' he said.

Phil and Helen made polite excuses and left shortly after Laura's scene. Mike sat alone in the living-room. He was angry with her and was definitely not inclined to follow her into the bedroom to talk things over.

After a few minutes, the bedroom door opened and Laura came out, looking rather sheepish. 'I heard them go,' she said quietly.

'Yes, well, you can pack just so many laughs into one evening,' Mike said bitterly, refusing to look at her.

Laura came and sat next to him. 'I'm sorry, Mike. It was childish.' Then she added quickly, 'I didn't say the word on purpose.'

Mike relented and put his arm around her. 'Oh, we've had it now – it will crop up all over the place. I bet the old film on television tonight is "Bringing Up Baby".'

'Anyway, I'm sorry. It's not fair to snipe at you in front of Helen and Phil. Just babyish – silly.'

'I didn't exactly jolly things along, did I, droning on about who gets the job?'

Laura smiled. 'We should have little cards printed. "Come round for a drink but on no account talk about yourselves." '

'Actually, I think I've solved that problem. I've decided.'

Laura immediately crossed her fingers.

'Which one are you crossing your fingers for?' he asked.

'Both of them.' Mike laughed. 'What?' She gave him a questioning look.

'Prophetic. I'm going to take both of them on.'

'You're not just being kind, are you?'

'No. I started thinking. I keep talking about expanding, but how can I expand when any time I get offered lots of work I'm too busy to handle it.'

Laura giggled. 'A personnel manager and a blue movie star.'

'Ex,' Mike corrected.

'It would take you to have a staff like that.'

'True.'

'This blue movie business,' she said thoughtfully. 'It is a bit yucky, isn't it?'

'I don't think he did it for fun. I think he did it for his little girl.' Mike stopped – somehow he had succeeded in raising the subject again. 'Perhaps if we ran up and down the road shouting "Baby!" at the tops of our voices, we could really forget it,' he said.

'Oh dear.'

'What?'

'I haven't forgotten it, Mike.'

'Oh.'

'I apologized for turning it into my sole topic of conversation,' she explained.

Mike forced a smile. 'Wishful thinking on my part.'

'I'm afraid so.'

'It *was* John Paul Jones. I looked it up.'

Laura stood up. 'Let's go to bed,' she said gently.

Mike sensed a trap. 'Oh, now look . . .'

'To sleep.'

'Sorry.'

'It's between us now, isn't it?'

'Yes it is,' he said, wishing it weren't.

'I didn't mean it to be.'

'I know that. You might change your mind.'

'You might change yours.'

Mike got to his feet. 'Anyway,' he said with an optimism he didn't feel, 'we're bound to sort it out.'

'Yes. Oh yes.'

Together they went into the bedroom, their arms around each other.

9

The music was romantic, the lights were low and Phil felt it not unreasonable to kiss Helen, who was cuddled up beside him on the couch. Kissing his wife had never been a problem to Phil before, but then she had never been twenty weeks pregnant before, so he took great care as he leant over her to support his own weight with one hand on the arm of the couch.

'Thank you,' Helen said, savouring the kiss.

Phil smiled down at her. 'All part of the friendly service.'

'You never used to do press-ups when you kissed me.'

'Well, I don't want to squash him, do I?'

'Could you manage another one?' she asked, lifting up her face.

'A baby?'

'A kiss,' she laughed.

'Could I manage another one?' Phil said with bravado. His arm was slowly giving way under the weight of his body and he had to admit defeat. 'No, I couldn't. Sorry.' He collapsed back on to his side of the couch and rubbed his arm. 'I'll have to sit on the other side some nights, you know, or by the time he's born I'm going to have one enormously muscled arm.'

'You're very sure about "he", aren't you?' Helen said, wondering if Phil had some inside information on the subject.

'Oh yes,' Phil said proudly. 'William Beaumont Barker.'

'If we call him that and he hates rugby, he's not going to like us.'

'My arm's better.'

'Oh, good.'

He prepared himself for another energetic kiss but the doorbell rang and the tender moment was lost for ever.

'Oh!' Helen said in an irritated voice. 'Now who's that?'

Reluctantly Phil dragged himself to his feet. 'I'll give you three guesses,' he said as he crossed the room. He threw open the door and Helen heard him say unenthusiastically, 'Hello, Laura.'

Laura bustled in and, giving Phil a perfunctory smile, headed straight for Helen. Phil allowed himself a private scowl and was about to close the door when he realized that Laura was not alone. Looking rather sheepish, Mike was hanging back down the garden path.

'Sorry, Mike,' Phil apologized.

'That's all right,' Mike said, stepping inside and giving Phil an uneasy smile. He knew that their sudden, unannounced visit was something of an intrusion. 'Look, we're not disturbing you, are we?' he asked.

'No,' Helen said kindly. 'Phil was only doing his antenatal exercises.'

Laura took off her coat and settled herself down on the sofa next to her sister. She reached into her bag and produced a gaily wrapped parcel. 'I bought a little present for the baby, and as we were on the way home from work and practically passing your door . . .'

Mike, who was hovering awkwardly behind the sofa, described three points of a triangle in the air with his finger – two very close, the third some way away. 'Office – our flat – your house,' he said. 'We always go the long way home.'

Laura stiffened visibly but didn't comment on this.

'Laura, you mustn't keep buying things,' Helen said. 'What is it?' she asked, intrigued despite herself.

She started to untie the ribbon, but Laura couldn't contain her patience, and snatched the parcel back. Excitedly she tore off the wrapping. 'It's a baby bouncer,' she announced.

'I didn't think you were supposed to bounce babies,' Phil said.

'Thank you, Laura – it's sweet,' Helen said, giving her a kiss.

Phil leant over to take a closer look at the contraption. 'What do you do with it?' he asked.

Laura was more than happy to demonstrate and took it back from Helen. 'You suspend it from a door frame or something and the baby sits in there and he can just bounce up and down to his heart's content.'

'He won't start ricocheting between the floor and the top of the door frame, will he?' Phil joked.

'Of course he won't,' Laura said, laughing up at him.

'That's what *I* said,' Mike commented.

'And I said the same thing to you,' Laura snapped, turning round to give him a glare.

'Except you didn't laugh,' Mike reminded her.

Laura pursed her lips. It was fairly obvious by now that there was a suppressed tension between them. Helen had been aware of it for some time, but even Phil, who was generally unobservant when it came to things like this, couldn't help but notice. Feeling that a diversionary tactic was called for, Helen asked if they'd care for a drink.

'Yes please,' Laura said. 'Sherry would be nice.'

'No thanks,' Mike said, still standing within reach

of the door, as if he were ready to go at a moment's notice.

'It is dry, isn't it?' Phil asked Laura as he started to pour her drink.

'I don't want one on my own,' Laura complained. It was a complaint directed specifically at Mike.

'I'll have one with you,' Phil offered. 'Are you sure, Mike?'

'Yes, thanks. I think we'd better be getting off, actually,' he said, edging closer to the door.

Laura took her drink from Phil. 'I am allowed to drink this first, am I?' she enquired sarcastically.

Mike sighed a long sigh. 'I meant when you'd finished it.'

'Well, why don't you have one?' Laura insisted.

'Because I don't want one,' he said, slowly and carefully, as though talking to a fractious child.

'I'll have one,' Helen said. 'Lemonade on the rocks please.'

'Right,' Phil said. He fixed Helen's drink and poured one for himself. 'Are you sure, Mike?'

'Yes. I'm driving and I had a pint at lunchtime.'

'A half, actually,' Laura corrected sourly. 'You had a half.'

'I had a pint.'

'You had a half.'

Phil interceded. 'It doesn't really matter, does it?'

'No,' Laura said, in the tone of voice that indicated that it mattered a great deal.

'No,' Mike said, looking grim.

'Cheers!' Helen said, raising her glass.

Everyone except Mike sipped their drinks dutifully.

'I just don't happen to think that half a pint of beer is worth being pedantic about,' Laura said, returning to the argument like a dog searching for a half-buried bone.

'Neither do I,' Mike said tersely.

'Oh, you admit it was a half.'

'No.'

'I said "half" and you said "neither do I".'

'I meant the half-pint difference between what you claim I had to drink and the pint I know I drank.'

Phil and Helen, the unwilling spectators of this inane quarrel, exchanged wary glances. A cheery evening was obviously not in prospect.

'I've never been so glad to see the back of those two in my life,' Phil said, as he and Helen prepared themselves a snack supper in the kitchen later that evening. 'And don't you defend them.'

'I wasn't going to. I was thinking of moving.'

'What is wrong with them lately?'

'Laura wants a baby and Mike doesn't,' Helen said, trying to keep the facts simple.

'Oh. I thought they'd dropped the idea.'

'Mike has and Laura hasn't.'

'Well, it takes two. That must be the end of it.'

'Mike hopes so and Laura doesn't.'

'You can't go on flogging a dead horse.'

'Laura will and Mike won't.'

'Have they talked it right through?'

'Mike thinks so and Laura doesn't.'

'No wonder they couldn't agree on how much beer he had at lunchtime.'

Helen, who had been trying to keep things on a light level, suddenly looked depressed. 'It's my fault,' she said.

'Oh, come on!'

'Well, I brought them together in the first place.'

'Yes, but they defied all the odds by staying together,' Phil pointed out in her defence. 'I just wish they'd sort out their problems together instead of coming round here and annoying us with them.'

'I know, but this . . .' Helen tried for a moment to put herself in Laura's shoes. 'What would we have done if I'd wanted a baby and you hadn't?'

'But I did.'

'Well, what if you'd wanted one and I hadn't?' Helen said, trying to simplify matters.

'But you did.'

'*If* I hadn't.'

'Well, if you hadn't and I hadn't . . .'

'No, if you had and I hadn't. Or . . .'

'They've done it again, haven't they?' Phil said. 'One hour listening to their gibberish and we end up talking gibberish to each other.'

'Gibber, gibber,' Helen said, and gave him a playful kiss.

'Well, now you're gibbering,' Phil said, putting his sandwich down and taking a bite out of her instead.

After Mike and Laura got back home, the row had escalated rapidly. It was in round six that they very nearly came to blows. In the circumstances, Laura decided that she couldn't possibly sleep in the same room as Mike and she made up her bed on the couch in the living-room.

It was half past two – that dead time of the night when everything seems at its most depressing. Laura couldn't get to sleep and tossed and turned fretfully. The couch, always so comfortable when it came to a cosy afternoon nap, now felt like a bed of nails.

She heard Mike stumbling about in the darkened room. He stubbed his toe on something and swore out loud. Laura sat up and switched on the table lamp.

'What are you creeping about for?' she demanded.

'I came to see if you were asleep.'

'I'm not now.'

'Before, I mean.'

She considered lying to make him feel bad, but settled for the truth. 'No, as a matter of fact.'

Mike sat down and rubbed his injured toe. 'I'm sure that furniture knows when someone's coming in the dark. It's my theory it moves itself about.'

She wasn't in the mood for light conversation. 'You didn't come out just to stub your toe, did you? she said coldly.

'No. Look, this is silly. Just because we have a row doesn't mean we can't share the same bed.'

'Are you taking back what you said?' she asked, still smarting from the unfair things he had said and determined to get an apology from him.

'Oh, for goodness' sake! We're not in the school playground!'

'Do you?'

'No.'

'Right!' She turned away from him and pulled the blanket up round her ears.

Mike started to go back towards the bedroom, but then paused. 'Then *I* should sleep on the couch,' he said.

'Why?' Laura asked, sticking her head up over the blanket.

'Well . . . because it's traditional.'

He went over to the couch and started to take the blanket from her. 'Come on. You have the bed.'

Laura held on to the blanket grimly. 'I don't want the bed!' she said petulantly, determined now to remain on her bed of nails just to punish him.

'Don't be silly!'

'Huh!'

Mike gave another yank on the blanket. Laura yanked it back.

'Let go of the blanket!' he ordered.

The struggle became fiercer and eventually, by

sheer force, Mike won possession. 'Ah!' he said, stepping back and waving his prize victoriously in the air. Laura got off the couch and advanced towards him. He dodged nimbly past her and jumped on to the couch, clutching the blanket to his chest.

'Now go to bed,' he told her.

'Would you get off that sofa, please? I want to sleep on the sofa.'

'No, you don't want to sleep on the sofa.'

'I do. Now get off.'

'No. I am sleeping on the sofa and that's an end to it.'

Laura knew that Mike had the physical advantage and she couldn't regain her territory by force, but she was determined that, if she couldn't sleep on the couch, neither would he.

'Very well,' she said in an ominously calm voice, and walked into the kitchen. There was the sound of running water and she re-entered the living-room, carefully holding a bowl.

Mike looked at the bowl of water and then at her face. 'Laura!' he warned.

He thought she might be bluffing, but she wasn't. She advanced towards the couch and hurled the contents of the bowl over him. He held the blanket up over his head, but it afforded no real protection and he was drenched.

'Sleep well,' she said, and marched into the bedroom. She got into bed and pulled the sheets around her. For a while, all was quiet and then she heard a familiar sound. She froze. The door opened and Mike came in carrying the bowl. She sat bolt upright.

'You wouldn't dare!'

But he would. He slowly poured the water over her, soaking the bed and the sheets. Trying to maintain her dignity, she got off the bed and went out of the room. Mike waited, somewhat apprehensively. She returned almost immediately with two large towels and tossed one of them to Mike.

'Perhaps we should have done this weeks ago,' she said calmly.

After they'd dried themselves and changed their clothes, Mike made them both a hot drink and they went to sit down in the living-room.

'I was going to hit you, you know,' Laura told him.

'I know.'

'Would you have hit me back?'

'Yes.'

'Really?'

'Yes.'

'Would you?' she asked again, finding it hard to believe.

'I never thought we'd end up sitting here at three o'clock in the morning talking about hitting each other,' Mike said miserably.

'Where did you think we'd end up?'

'I don't know. Nowhere, for a long time – then somewhere – together,' he said vaguely.

'But not with a child?'

This constant harping on about babies was beginning to get him down. He gave her a warning look.

'I'm talking about it, Mike,' Laura said. 'I'm not niggling or naggling – nagging. I'm talking about it quietly and sensibly and I promise it's for the last time.'

Mike considered this for a long while, then said carefully, 'If I thought . . .'

'Yes?' Laura said eagerly.

'If I thought we could look after a baby – bring it up . . .'

'Of course we could!' She was beginning to feel that Mike was coming round to her point of view – perhaps there was some hope after all.

'You need to be responsible. You need to be settled.'

'Well, we are.'

'Ten minutes ago we were throwing buckets of water over each other. Now is that the action of responsible adults?'

'You'd make a lovely father,' Laura said, smiling at him softly.

'I don't know why you think that,' he said, frowning.

'Because you're kind.'

'Oh, very kind. Going around hitting women. That's very kind.'

'You didn't hit me,' she reminded him.

'I would have done.'

'Only if I'd hit you first. I thought of it first.'

'What if a child had been watching that?'

'If we had a child, we wouldn't have done it.' She felt she was losing ground and was beginning to get too emotional.

'There you go again,' Mike said. 'A baby is just a baby. It's not some magic that cures everything that's wrong between two people.'

'What do you mean, "everything"? Everything isn't wrong,' she said desperately.

'I know. I didn't think anything was wrong. I thought we were doing rather well. I thought we were starting to enjoy each other.'

'We were.'

'Well, why have a baby to put everything right when everything is right without a baby in the first place?'

She'd lost. She knew it. Mike had found the fatal flaw in her argument.

'It doesn't mean to say that things couldn't get better,' she said.

'No,' he agreed, though he looked doubtful at this.

'I'm thinking of us, Mike,' she pleaded.

'You're not.'

'You mean I'm selfish?'

'No, but it's not us that wants a baby.'

'If we had a son, you could teach him the business.'

'Oh, he'd love that,' Mike scoffed. ' "Son – give up all thoughts of being a rich merchant banker. Dad is going to teach you how to be a struggling landscape gardener." '

'You won't always be struggling. You're good at it and word gets round.'

'Well, I wish it would hurry up. I'm not getting any younger.' This gave him further ammunition. 'And that's another thing – we're too old.'

Laura felt she was on safe ground here. 'Medically speaking . . .'

'Not medically speaking – practically speaking. We could die before the child grew up.'

'Oh, now that's downright morbid.'

'Well, I certainly couldn't kick a football around.'

'Of course you could.'

'I couldn't. If one of my sticks slipped, I'd go flat on my back.' He was hoping this might raise a smile, but it didn't.

'Is it because you didn't have a mother and father?'

'Of course I had a mother and father. I didn't arrive in a capsule from the planet Krypton!'

'Not knowing them, I mean.'

'I don't know,' he said tiredly.

'I'm not budging you, am I?' she said sadly.

'It's like spending money on double-glazing while the roof's still leaking.'

Laura could think of nothing further to say. 'Then I think we'd better get some sleep,' she said.

'The bed's soaked, the sofa's soaked and we've only got one dry blanket left. We'd better make our rows dry ones from now on.' Mike got to his feet and tucked the blanket around Laura. 'There you are.' He switched the light off and settled himself down in his own chair.

Laura got up almost immediately and cuddled up on Mike's lap, pulling the blanket over both of them. 'Goodnight, Mike,' she said.

'Goodnight, Laura.' He stroked her damp hair and closed his eyes. Laura felt exhausted but she was past sleep, and for a long time she stared unseeingly into the dark.

Mike woke up to the realization that he had severe neckache. Painfully he creaked to his feet and found he had severe backache as well. Laura had obviously got up before him, and he wandered around the flat looking for her. She was nowhere to be found. The more he thought about her absence, the more alarmed he became. The only place he thought she might be was Phil and Helen's. It was a long shot, but worth checking out, so he dialled the number.

Phil answered with a sleepy grunt.

'Phil? Good morning, it's Mike. Sorry to be a bit early. . . . Is it really as early as that?' He checked his watch. 'So it is. The thing is, Phil, I wondered if Laura was there? No, I don't see why she should be either, but she's not here, you see. No. She must be somewhere else, then. Yes. Sorry. I didn't wake you up, did I? Sorry. 'Bye, Phil.'

He dressed hurriedly and was just about to dash out of the flat to search for her when Laura came in. She was carrying a plastic laundry bag and a shopping bag.

'Hello, Mike,' she said wanly.

'Where have you been?'

'To the launderette.'

'I was coming to look for you.'

'Why?'

'Because you weren't here.'

'No, I was in the launderette.'

'We've established that. What were you doing there?'

'Drying the wet bedclothes.'

'It's seven o'clock,' he said, pointing to his watch.

'I didn't sleep very well.'

'Neither did I, but I didn't get up and sneak off to the launderette!' His relief at finding her safe was turning to anger.

'I didn't sneak off anywhere,' she said quietly.

'You get some pretty weird people in launderettes at odd hours.'

'What weird people?'

'Well, for a start. . .'

Laura didn't want to pursue the matter. 'What about some breakfast?' she suggested.

'Yes, all right,' Mike said, realizing as soon as he'd said it that that he didn't feel particularly hungry after the upsets of the previous day.

'What would you say to egg, bacon, sausage, mushrooms and tomatoes?' she asked brightly.

'Not a lot.'

She looked disappointed at this. 'But you like a cooked breakfast.'

'Not this morning. Just a cup of tea and a piece of toast will be fine.'

'I think you should have a cooked breakfast,' she insisted.

He looked puzzled. 'Why?'

'Because I'd like to cook one for you.'

It seemed a peculiar reason to Mike. 'Does sleeping in a chair always make you behave like this?'

'Just tea and toast,' she said, and went into the kitchen.

The telephone rang and Mike went to answer it. It

was Helen, who had obviously received a garbled version of Mike's previous telephone call from Phil. She was worried, and Mike had to explain that Laura was quite safe and had only gone to the launderette. Helen rang off decidedly more confused than before.

Laura, who had overheard a bit of the conversation, asked, 'Why did you phone Helen?'

'I thought you might have gone round there.'

'At seven o'clock in the morning?'

'That's far more likely than going to a launderette at seven o'clock in the morning!' he snapped.

'Oh, don't by angry, Mike. Not this morning.'

'I'm not angry – just a bit confused.' He suddenly noticed Laura's shopping bag. 'That bag is full of food,' he said.

'I went shopping as well – while the things dried.'

'I see.'

'Well, it never does any harm to stock up, does it?'

'No, I suppose not. This isn't going to be a way of life is it, this dawn activity?'

Laura smiled. 'I shouldn't think so.' She brought the toast in from the kitchen, and they sat down at the table to eat their meagre breakfast.

Laura looked at Mike intently. 'We've had a lot more good times than bad, haven't we?' she asked, unexpectedly.

'Yes, of course we have. Why?'

'It's just nice to know that, isn't it?'

'Yes, I suppose it is,' Mike said, although he hadn't given it much thought.

It was a strange question, but then Laura's behaviour that morning seemed very strange – eccentric, even. He decided to put it down to their rough night, and took another bite out of his toast. He looked up and caught her staring at him strangely. 'Have I got marmalade somewhere?' he asked, wiping his chin.

'No,' she said, looking away hastily.

'Are you all right?'

'Me? I'm fine.'

'You look peculiar.'

'Thank you.'

'Not peculiar. Funny.'

'Perhaps my early start is catching up with me.' She took a deep breath. 'Look, Mike, I shan't be coming to the office today.'

He could understand this – they both needed a little time to themselves to recover emotionally. 'No, all right,' he said.

'I've got some things to catch up on.'

'Yes, of course. You haven't let your translating slip by helping me out, have you?'

'No, I can pick that up any time. Actually, now you've taken on Mr Robinson and Terry, I don't really think you'll need me in the office.'

'I wouldn't say that.'

'I mean, I have seen Mr Robinson type. He's much faster than I am – not so messy either.'

'It's funny that we both call him Mr Robinson,' Mike observed.

'I just can't bring myself to call him Wilfred.'

'Neither can I,' he said, smiling.

'What does young Terry call him?'

'Wilf.'

She laughed. 'He would. Still, they're nice people, aren't they, both of them?'

'Oh yes. Once each of them learns to understand what the other is talking about, they'll make a good team.'

'I'm glad you're working with nice people.'

'They like you,' Mike said.

'Nice people with good taste.' She picked up the teapot. 'More tea?'

'No thanks. I might as well get off, actually – set the staff a good example.'

This was the moment, then. Laura dreaded Mike leaving, but there was nothing she could do to stop him without making him even more suspicious than he already was. She helped him on with his coat. 'I'm sorry about last night, Mike.'

'So am I.'

'We won't think of it as typical, will we?'

'I shouldn't think so. We've never chucked water over each other before.'

'True.'

'Right, then,' he said as cheerfully as he could. 'I'm off to brutalize the workers. Cheerio.'

'Cheerio, Mike.' She kissed him and watched him walk out of the front door. She stood there for a while before turning back into the living-room. She was very close to tears now, but fought them back. 'Come on,' she said, urging herself on, and she went into the bedroom.

Just lately, Phil and Helen had given up reading the newspapers at the breakfast table. No journalism – no matter how sensational – could overshadow the strange comings and goings of Mike and Laura.

'To the launderette?' Phil said, looking sceptical.

'Yes.'

'At seven o'clock in the morning?'

'That's what Mike said – unless I misheard him. No, I couldn't have done. I can't think of another word that sounds like "launderette", can you?'

Phil made a brave try, but couldn't. 'Not really,' he agreed. 'You don't think she's finally gone round the twist, do you?' With Laura it wasn't something you could rule out that easily.

'That's my sister you're talking about,' Helen said.

As if on cue, the doorbell rang. Phil and Helen looked at each other.

'No,' Helen said.

'Do you want to bet?' Phil said grimly as he got up to answer the door.

He was right. Laura was standing there. The second and third things he noticed were two suitcases.

'They're suitcases,' she said, following his gaze.

'You're not thinking of moving in, are you?' he asked.

'Don't worry,' she said. Phil helped her in with the cases and closed the door. Helen came out from the kitchen to see who it was. 'They're cases,' she said immediately.

'We've already established that,' Phil said.

'You're not . . .?'

'No,' Laura said wearily.

'What *are* you doing?' Phil asked.

'I'm going to Brussels, you see. I'm sure I can get a job there. All those Euro MPs shouting at each other in their own languages – they must wear out interpreters very quickly.'

'What about Mike?' Helen asked.

'He doesn't need an interpreter,' Laura said flippantly, deliberately misunderstanding the question.

'Laura, don't be silly. You know what I mean.'

'You can't go charging off to Brussels every time you have a row,' Phil said.

'If I'd done that lately,' Laura said, smiling rue-fully, 'I'd never have been off an aeroplane.'

'What did Mike say?' Helen asked.

'Nothing. I didn't tell him.' She suddenly felt a bit sick and sat down suddenly on the couch.

Helen sat down beside her. 'You mean you just walked out?'

'No, I saw Mike off to work – he wouldn't have a

big fry-up for breakfast – then I packed, and now I'm going to the airport.'

'Oh, that's charming,' Phil said bitterly.

'You left him a note?' Helen asked.

'No.'

'So he gets home tonight. No you – no note. He'll start worrying,' Phil said.

'He'll phone here, I expect,' Laura said.

'Yes, he probably . . .' Phil suddenly caught on. 'You've got a nerve!'

'I couldn't tell him,' Laura said sadly. 'And I can't write notes. What could I put in a note?'

It was a rhetorical question, but Phil had an answer.' "Dear Mike, I'm ratting on you." '

'I'm not.'

'All right, doing the dirty on you.'

Laura looked to her sister for comfort and advice.

'You should have told him,' Helen said gently.

'I couldn't. He'd have made a long, beautiful speech like "Don't go" and I'd have stayed. And what good would that have done? We'd try because we like each other, but we can't solve this one – it won't go away and we'd end up not liking each other and that would be worse.' It was a pretty garbled explanation, but to Phil and Helen, who were Mike and Laura pundits, it made some kind of sense. Laura got to her feet. 'So. May I ring for a taxi?'

'No, we'll take you to the airport, won't we Phil?'

'Yes, of course,'

'Thanks.' Laura smiled at them gratefully. 'I'll just . . .' she said, and ran upstairs. Helen waited until she was out of earshot and then rushed over to the phone. Feverishly, she started to dial.

'Who are you ringing?' Phil asked suspiciously.

'Mike.'

'Oh, no, you don't!' He crossed to the phone and held the receiver rest down firmly with his finger.

'If he gets to the airport and she sees him. . .' Helen said, ever the romantic.

'Helen, you've got to let go of those two. Carry on like this and we'll end up adopting them.'

'They love each other.'

'Like. She said "like".'

'What if she's silly in Brussels?' Helen said dramatically.

'She's silly everywhere.'

'Phil!'

'Oh, come on! She's not going to end up haunting the waterfront bars in a plastic mac, with a fag in her mouth.'

'There isn't a waterfront in Brussels.'

'Seriously, maybe it's for the best. I've often thought that the only thing those two really have got in common is having nothing in common.'

'Being lonely,' Helen said.

'True.'

At that moment Laura came downstairs, putting a stop to any further discussion.

'You'll look after Mike, won't you?' she said.

'Yes.' Phil nodded. 'He can sleep in the nursery till the baby arrives.'

'I'm ready, then,' Laura said, and started to pick up her cases.

'I'll take those,' Phil said, and carried them to the door. Laura opened the door for him and they started to leave.

Helen made as if to follow them and then stopped suddenly. 'I think I'll need a coat,' she said. 'I won't be a minute.' She waited until they were halfway down the path and then dashed to the telephone. She started to dial Mike's number with shaking fingers.

'Helen!' a warning voice said and, looking up, Helen saw Laura standing at the door, watching her.

She smiled weakly. Carefully she put the reciever back on the hook and followed Laura out of the house.

By tacit consent, there was no further mention of Mike, and the conversation was strictly confined to small talk and travel generalities. It placed a considerable strain on everyone, and when the time came for Laura to go through to the departure lounge there was a sense of relief mingled with the sadness.

As Phil and Helen walked away, Helen had a little cry. Phil put a comforting arm around her and held her close for a while. Helen buried her head in his shoulder and, when she looked up, she was surprised to see Mike rushing towards them.

'Never delayed when you want them to be, are they, planes?' he said, trying to catch his breath.

'How did you know?' Helen asked.

'Phil phoned.'

She looked at Phil for an explanation. 'We had to stop for petrol, remember?'

Helen smiled up at him – she was grateful that he had tried. 'I'm sorry, Mike,' she said.

'Well,' he shrugged, 'Brussels isn't far.'

'You're going to catch the next plane, aren't you?' she said, hoping for a happy ending after all.

'No. I just meant that Brussels isn't very far if. . .' he broke off. 'Perhaps it is,' he said dejectedly.

As they walked slowly out of the airport terminal, Helen put her arm through Mike's.

'Are you on a yellow line?' Phil asked.

'Yes.'

'Double yellow line?'

'Oh, yes,' Mike said.

*

Laura took a last look at London Airport before the plane, circling higher, broke through the clouds. The 'No smoking' signs flashed off. The man sitting next to Laura turned and offered her a cirgarette. She smiled and shook her head. The last person to offer her a cigarette had been Mike, when he was doing his bad impersonation of Paul Henreid – and look where that had led.

BESTSELLING FICTION FROM ARROW

All these books are available from your bookshop or news-agent or you can order them direct. Just tick the titles you want and complete the form below.

THE DEFECTOR	Evelyn Anthony	£1.75
THE HISTORY MAN	Malcolm Bradbury	£1.75
1985	Anthony Burgess	£1.75
THE BILLION DOLLAR KILLING	Paul Erdman	£1.75
THE YEAR OF THE FRENCH	Thomas Flanagan	£2.50
EMMA SPARROW	Marie Joseph	£1.60
COCKPIT	Jerzy Kosinski	£1.60
CITY OF THE DEAD	Herbert Lieberman	£1.75
STRUMPET CITY	James Plunkett	£2.50
TO GLORY WE STEER	Alexander Kent	£1.75
TORPEDO RUN	Douglas Reeman	£1.50
THE BEST MAN TO DIE	Ruth Rendell	£1.25
SCENT OF FEAR	Margaret Yorke	£1.25
2001: A SPACE ODYSSEY	Arthur C. Clarke	£1.75
THE RUNNING YEARS	Claire Rayner	£2.50
	Postage	
	Total	

ARROW BOOKS, BOOKSERVICE BY POST, PO BOX 29, DOUGLAS, ISLE OF MAN, BRITISH ISLES

Please enclose a cheque or postal order made out to Arrow Books Limited for the amount due including 10p per book for postage and packing for orders within the UK and 12p for overseas orders.

Please print clearly

NAME ....

ADDRESS ....

....

Whilst every effort is made to keep prices down and to keep popular books in print, Arrow Books cannot guarantee that prices will be the same as those advertised here or that the books will be available.